GW01457844

Beneath Your Watchful Eyes

by

Jane Bowyer

PUBLISH AMERICA

PublishAmerica
Baltimore

First printing

ISBN: 1-4137-6354-5
PUBLISHED BY PUBLISHAMERICA, LLLP
www.publishamerica.com
Baltimore

Printed in the United States of America

For Simon

Acknowledgments

With many thanks to everyone that has helped in any way with this book.

Special thanks to Simon for his support.

Thanks Karla and Jason for your friendship. To Chris for answering my questions. To Peter and Renee Mouse for their reading and love. To John for his encouraging appraisal, and Liz and Katherine for the wonderful photography. To all my extended family, who are too many to name, but that have had to put up with me over the years, and despite my obsession for my dream and my lack of spare time have accepted that I needed to do this.

To Abigail and anyone else who is just starting out on their journey … may it be safe and full of love.

A Life-changing Experience
Sept 11, 2001

I can't remember his name, but if I were to copy that guy out of the *Fight Club* movie ... do you know the one? There isn't anything wrong with him, he just likes to go along and listen to other people's problems to enable him to get a good night's sleep! This seems to be a little desperate, but as I have never had any difficulty in sleeping, I guess I don't know how it feels to have insomnia as badly as he does. So if I were to do the same as he, I would probably introduce myself to everyone as, *"Hi, my name is Eric Morrison. I'm only thirty-three years of age and I have had and lost everything. I have an addiction, but it's not exactly the norm. My dependency isn't to be put down to drugs or drink. Though I do like to drink more than I should, and I love cocaine. But my drugs aren't regular, as it's like everything else in this world; it is always down to how much money I have in the pot and that is something I never know from one day to the next. I have a problem, you see, that's darker than words can describe. I'd have to tell you the whole story before you can understand what I mean. It's the only way you can get to know the real me.*

Some of the group might say to me, "Well, Mr. Morrison, at least you have admitted you have a problem—at least you have made the first step. We do understand already, Mr. Morrison. If you are willing to be honest, then we are willing to help." Perhaps some of the group may empathise with my pain a little too much, and especially the woman might start to cry. Soon there might be lots of tears and the, "it's OK to cry" view would sweep the room. Kleenex would be passed around. Everyone would be far too involved with this special moment to notice that I am unable to cry.

The reality is that until recently I would rather have boiled my feet than talk about what happened and I don't think I have been able to cry since I was about eight years of age. Even when I was being frog-marched into the police station I didn't want to talk. Even when I was cleared in the court room I still didn't talk. The fat lawyers and solicitors did that for me and rightfully took a fat cut of my fortune before I pissed most of the rest of it all away.

I am a coward—I will admit that. Well, it's not even that, really. I just can't be bothered anymore. There are set rules in modern life— set ways of thinking—and I defy them all! No, I never grew out of the rebellious teenage thing.

As it stands I live in North London (not trendy Islington or cultural Stoke Newington. Not even up and coming Dalston). No, I live on a street that no one's ever heard of just off the Caledonian Road. My building is sandwiched between the crack dealers on the right and the arguing pimps of the unofficial massage parlour on the left. If you were passing my building during the day you would describe it as nice. It's Georgian with great big sash windows and steps up to the front door. It's three old houses knocked into one. It's not sure if it's a hotel or bed and breakfast. There is a sandwich shop opposite which serves great coffee and around the corner is a Tesco's supermarket and an OK pub down the road. It could be classed as OK, but just wait until after dark when the buildings either side start to wake up. Things get interesting then. The inside of this hotel is crummier than can be imagined. Like I said, it's not really a hotel but rather a building for guys like me to live permanently because we don't have anywhere else to go. The rooms are small, but I'm lucky to have my own bath and toilet. It's the only ensuite in the hotel and the only reason I got the thing was because the last tenant died of a heart attack and I came along on the day they were removing the body. It was one of those cases you read about in the newspaper when the poor man was dead for a month before anyone smelt him. The owner told me that the man liked to clean his own room, that is why no one missed him. We're not allowed to clean our own rooms now.

"We'll have to charge you an extra five pounds a week for the bathroom and we'll need two months deposit up front," Fat Georg had demanded as I moved in. Sweat had poured onto his chest as he did nothing but watch me struggle to move the dirty mattress that they had the nerve to call a bed.

"How about this Rolex instead?" I had negotiated. Of course the thing was an expensive fake, but not so the ordinary person could tell. I had stolen it—but at the time I didn't really have any choice, and besides, the person who owned it was bad to the bones.

"Sure, but don't expect me to give you it back," he told me as he scratched at his fat arse.

"Georg, I hope it brings you more luck then it has brought me." I laughed

"Oh, it will, believe me, it will!" He chuckled, swaying his coffee so that droplets splashed out and burnt me on the face. As soon as I was alone I slung that mattress straight out of the window and then went down to Argos to order a new one.

I now have my new bed right by the window. It's there so that I can watch London go by in its usual chaotic mess. Who needs television when there is so much more to see in the real world? Today there is a couple having an argument in the street. A late summer shower is pouring from the sky, but they don't seem to notice. From the look of them both they should call it a day, as it always ends in tears. I've been through shit like this and when it turns ugly I can't see why people still bother. But they can't just walk away as there are complications. She's pregnant, but not wearing a wedding ring. He, on the other hand, has a band boldly across his finger. They are well in the shit. He probably has a wife at home right now cutting carrots in some big house, blissfully unaware that her husband has been fucking his work colleague for the last year. I bet he told her he is away on business. The guy is starting to get aggressive; he waves his hands at her face as if it's all her fault. She runs across the road to get away from him, passes right by my window. She's attractive, but over-made up. He tries to follow her, but car after car prevents him reaching her. Finally he gets a break, but it's too late as she's jumped on a bus. The traffic clears and she is gone—there's no chance of him catching her now. He shouts at the air for a bit, but then gets into his BMW and drives out of my life.

Nothing much happens after that until Rachel's new single erupts from the radio and it puts me down in the dumps. The first day I manage to tune the temperamental thing and she's on it. The song is shit, just like life. Her vocals are pathetic, just like the month, drab old end-of-the-summer September, with the anniversary of the day it went all wrong for me squashed right in the middle of it. I fucking hate this month. It just reminds me of how little I have come on in the last year. A bold voice in my head keeps at me, asking me again and again, every bloody minute, *Eric, what's the point of all this trying when reality is nothing more than camping out with a broken television and a six pack of lager? Nothing is going to change now so why try?* I can see his point.

"You need a complete lifestyle change." That is what Dr. West told me back in the day when I could afford a therapist. "You are your own biggest problem," he said as I had sat for the first time in his leather chair as he pretended to listen to me foolishly pour out my life with the sad delusion that he had my best interest at heart. All the fucker had to say was, "All your troubles are a direct result of the way you conduct your life. The image you have in your head of your standing in society is not the same as how everyone else sees you. Mr. Morrison, you have filled your days with superficial emptiness. You are throwing your life away and it's no surprise that you feel unfulfilled for doing so. In short, despondency has caused you to have this breakdown." He picked at his nose, drilled his finger right in there as if I wasn't in the room.

"I can't see how that can be true …" I had protested. "I'm not a lazy man."

"I think you are missing the point, Mr. Morrison. It's your lifestyle that's the main contributor to your drug addiction."

I switched off after this point. Like I said earlier, I liked my drugs and drinks, but that wasn't the problem. He was so wrong, for at the time, way back then, the reason I was like I was wasn't anything to do with self-image and all that crap—no, it was all Rachel's fault. She's the one who got into my world and pulled it away from under me.

Now I move at my own pace. I can take ten minutes to make a sandwich and notice all the unimportant things, like how many times the house opposite opens and closes their blinds during the day time and also how many times the Turkish couple in the room next door to me shag. I even take ages to clean my teeth, make sure that no surface is missed. Plaque cannot breed in my mouth.

There is a program about Arsenal soccer team about to start on cable so I leave my crappy portable and head to the communal TV room to watch the, still crap, but big, TV that sits in all its ten-year-old glory sandwiched between two lime green pillars. I have to keep my mind active, they tell me. TV is good. Heroine would be better— if only I wasn't scared of needles.

The room is down two flights of stairs and the whole time I have lived here I have never seen anyone else walking down these stairs at the same time as me. There are fifty rooms in this place, so how come no one else seems to be about? Are they all prisoners to Fat Georg? Forced to lick his armpits in exchange for the rent? If that's the case, then I'm glad I gave him the Rolex!

The second I get in there, I want to walk straight out again. MTV is on the television and Rachel is singing. Some lazy bastard has left it on. That is one of the rules in this place; never leave the TV on. Rachel looks great. Bad thing, really—bad thing to hear and see her twice in one day. Nothing for months and then twice in one day!

No one makes an appearance, so I watch the soccer program. To add to the room's negative décor, it also has the disadvantage of smelling like old people and the high-backed chair I'm sitting on has seen better days. This is also true about the whole place, including myself, and probably the rest of the residence. Have I really got at least forty years left of this? The highlight of my day, watching TV alone. I can't imagine life beyond that at the moment. I can't plan anything other than the now.

I want to score, but instead I have to console with watching Arsenal do so instead—beautiful. As I cheer, a girl comes in. She's wearing scruffy jeans and her hair is piled on the top of her head as if she is trying to get it as far away from her face as she possibly can. Her body is good. I slurp my beer by accident, trying to get a look at her face.

"Excuse me, sir, but you will have to vacate the room while I clean it," she says in a surprising Spanish accent. She is sweating and I'm surprised, because if she is Spanish then how the hell is she so hot in rainy old England?

"You can clean around me, can't you?" I say as her blue eyes glare at me.

"Come on, get out. You can come back in five minutes when the place is clean, or you can help me, but I'm not vacuuming around a man who has nothing better to do then watch TV during the day."

I feel like pointing out to her that she is nothing more than a maid who cleans up shit after people in the crummiest hotel in the world. But I like her. I can see that beyond the bad clothes and unmade face there is someone who is a little bit more than just a maid. So I do as she tells me and stand outside the room as she cleans the place.

I'm smoking my tenth cigarette of the day when she screams at the top of her voice.

"Nooooo! Beer man come in here right now! No!" I'm in two minds to listen, after all she mustn't get paid much here and perhaps she's some kind of nut case. Then, on the other hand, maybe she is naked and waiting for me to come and have sex with her.

I run straight in there.

She is kneeling before the TV, fully clothed, her hand touching at the screen.

"What's going on?" I ask, but she doesn't reply.

I watch in horror as the news repeats what appears to be a plane crashing into the twin towers in New York. First I think it's a film and then I hope it is.

"My God!" I say. "This doesn't look real."

But she isn't listening. She's crying.

"My brother works in that building—right near the top!" she tells me. Her tone is hysterical as snot unashamedly falls from her nose. "How are they going to get out of there? They are all going to die."

"They can save them. The army can help."

"How?" she asks and I'm at a loss for words by this time, for I don't have the answer. She stops crying. She sits silently as they repeat the first and second tower collapsing all through the night and still none of it seems real. It's just like a movie, but unlike a movie, the re-runs are just as devastating as the first time I saw them.

At six the next morning I have had it and I say to her, "Don't you want me to walk you home?"

"There is no need. I live here."

"Do you? What number?"

"38"

"You should go to bed now."

"He could still be alive. I have to wait until they check the rubble."

"They will, but not for a few hours. They need to all rest for a bit," I say, pulling her to her feet. "What's your name, by the way?"

"Luisa."

"Luisa, do yourself a favour and go and lie down for a bit."

"But I can't."

"You must do—if your brother is alive he will need you to be at your best. Go to bed, Luisa." I watch her as she reluctantly slopes off down the hallway. I watch her until she reaches her room.

The news, of course, never comes. They never find him, but he's dead all right, just like the other thousands of people who were murdered for the whole world to painfully see.

After that I don't see Luisa for a few weeks until I bump into her in the supermarket right next to the tomatoes and peppers. The organic section with its end-of-day reduced items.

"How you doing?" I ask, wondering if she still recognises me. Her face is tanned and I can only guess that she has been back in Spain all this time. Best to leave it, though, for I have never been any good around crying women and I don't want to make her blab again.

"Badly," she replies, "my mother wants me to move back to Spain in case they attack London."

"Do you want to go back?"

She screws up her face. "No, but my mother worries."

"Luisa, it's nice to be loved."

"I suppose it is," she replies, "but you don't know my mother! As much as I love her, she can drive me mad. She's always trying to fix me up with weird men. She thinks I should settle down and get married."

"Maybe you should listen to her," I tease, digging through the cabbages, but when I look up, Luisa has already gone off to pay for her shopping.

Baz Luhrmann Movie
End of October 2001

The next morning I purposely linger behind in my room. I want to speak to Luisa and I know if I stay in long enough that she will be due to clean my room.

At eleven thirty she comes in without knocking. Her face is flushed and she looks annoyed to see me there. What we had shared in the TV room seems to have been forgotten. Something so sad and unrepeatable has not made her even consider me as a friend. I sense she has a practicalness and isn't prone to such emotional outbursts like Rachel used to be. She's probably embarrassed for crying in front of me; I would be.

Draped around her small waist is an apron and on her hands is one green and one yellow rubber glove. She is a funny little woman who under certain light is almost pretty.

"You know the rules, Mr. Morrison, no guests in the room between ten and two," she says, stoning me with her words.

"How is your mother?"

She raises her eyes, but only to look at me. "I told you yesterday she wants me to move back to Spain."

"I'm not feeling great," I say, forcing out a pathetic cough.

"Well, I'm very sorry, but if you want your room cleaned out then you are going to have to leave." Her hands grip the back of her half-exposed back and I can see that her shoulders are as brown as a caramel. How I would like to lick that caramel.

"Let's say I help you," I offer, knowing that she isn't going to agree with me.

"Let's say you leave me to do the job I'm paid for. I don't know you that well and I don't feel comfortable cleaning with one of the guests watching me."

"Well, what if I told you about myself. Would that make it feel better for you?"

"If you want to talk and get to know a woman, Mr. Morrison, you need to go to a bar."

"But I want to get to know you."

"By watching me clean your toilet? I maybe a maid, Mr. Morrison, but you shouldn't presume things. I'm not stupid!"

"I never said you were."

"I'm only doing this for a short while to get some money instead of sitting on my backside all day like it appears you are doing. Now just because I'm poor doesn't mean I will jump into bed with the first good-looking man that offers me it."

So she likes me. She wouldn't be so defensive if she didn't like, even if it is just a little bit.

"Well, Luisa, just because I'm sitting on my backside doesn't mean I don't want to work. I can't, and when did I say I wanted to go to bed with you?" I want to make her feel stupid.

"Maybe not with your mouth, but your eyes told me so! Why can't you work? Are you useless or something?" she snaps, and I think her comment, no matter how well-delivered, is far too below the belt.

"There's a bit more to it, I'm afraid," I sulk. "I can't fucking help it."

"There always is, isn't there? Men will always find an excuse to be lazy."

"Believe that if you want to, but I'm not lazy."

"Maybe you aren't, but it is hardly good reason for me to get to know you or for you to try and impress me when all I have seen of you so far is you sitting inside drinking beer and watching TV." She started to dust the bedroom and I'm petrified that she will find my dope. She's getting close to it and has just to move my shirt from the chair and it's sitting there in a see-through bag. She might smoke it, but I don't want to take the risk as she might be one of these anti-drug girls and could call the police. I could do without the trouble, really. It's going to happen—she's going to find the bag as it's merely inches from her face.

"I haven't always been a bum you know," I say as she moves from the chair and bends down to clean the floor. I can sort of see down her top, but I daren't risk her catching me looking. However, she is too involved with her task to notice, so immediately I scrunch up the dope bag into my shirt and toss it into the cupboard. She doesn't notice. I'm a good shot.

"You don't say," she says, not really interested in what I've got to say.

"No, once I had a good job, a nice house, plenty of money, and a girlfriend. Then it all went wrong."

"Why, what did you do, have an affair with the wrong woman?" she smirks, helping herself to one of my cigarettes. What is it with woman stealing my fags?

"A bit worse than that. Maybe I will tell you about it sometime."

She stares at me. "I know all about you, Mr. Morrison. Everyone does in this place. Now I really need to do my work, so if you could clear out for half an hour."

"I'm going," I say, grabbing my jacket. I'm almost out of earshot when she shouts...

"Oh, by the way, I have tonight off."

"You do?"

"Yes, so if you would like to meet me outside at eight—I'll take you to a cheap club that I know. But only if you can pay for yourself. You can pay for yourself, can't you?"

"Sure," I say, leaving before she has a chance to change her mind.

I walk around the block and have a proper smoke. The day is cold and since it's a Friday, I don't feel much like looking for a job. I go back and watch monster trucks on Eurosport.

At seven thirty it starts to really piss down and I'm worried it will put Luisa off meeting me. Some girls won't come out if it rains. Strange, I know, but their hair is too complicated for the likes of water.

At five to eight I run out to wait for her, but she's already there standing in the doorway, puffing on a Camel.

"Come, Mr. Morrison, the rain is messing me up."

"I'm not late, am I?" I ask.

"Come. We can take the bus—if you sit upstairs at the back they don't always collect your fare. I warn you, though, my friends and the place can be a little crazy."

"Where we going?" I ask as we jump off at Soho.

"It's a surprise," she says.

Her description of the place is mild compared to the reality. A little crazy would be the words you might use to describe a hen night in Southampton, but this place, well, this place is right off the scale. I couldn't find it again if my life depended on it. It's twisted somewhere between Covent Garden and Soho, then down some steps behind a door, then up another flight of stairs—after that I can't remember. We only went there once.

This place surely could have only come from a dream. Brightly clothed people with faces made up like they had just stepped out of a Baz Luhrmann movie dance around the floor. The whole place is lit by candlelight and the bar has every kind of drink you could possibly want. Luisa makes me dance with her; I must look a bit of an idiot, but, hey, I don't care. She's a really good dancer. Not that I'm shit, but this is Spanish stuff and the way she moves in front of me transforms her from a cleaner to a Spanish princess. Her feet skim the floor and somehow I glide along with her in perfect time. I'm tripping and it feels great. I want to undress her right there and fuck her all night, but she wants another drink and I guess I can wait.

As we stand at the end of the bar, the way she talks makes me feel like I have known her for years. She has so much to say. I listen as she tells me of Spanish summers and how she sneaked into the country once, but has now got a work permit.

Ecstasy is a great drug. Everyone is in love on Ecstasy. The world is beautiful like the first dawn. She is sexy. I want tonight to last forever—for dawn to never come. I think I tell her this, for she laughs. Slowly she polishes off a jug of sangria before she decides she wants to go home.

"OK," I say as she takes my hand in hers.

"So you like the club, then?" she asked me as we opened the doors onto the raining night.

"Yes," I say. "Where's your coat, Luisa?"

"Someone stole it, I think."

"What, in there?"

"Yes."

"We should go back in and find it."

"It's gone—the girl on the cloakroom did a runner with the money and took my coat with it."

"We should call the police, then."

"The place shouldn't be there. The police are not an option."

"But you will catch a cold."

"You can keep me warm, Eric."

And I do, that night and the next night until in the end it feels like Luisa has always been about.

Cero—The Godfather of N1
December 2001

Luisa decides over a breakfast burrito that to enable me to gain some of my self-respect back and to also have a chance of getting some sort of life that is worth having, I should stop living off my dole cheque and become a real man by earning my way. She didn't quite put it that way, but in the heat of an argument more extreme words were used.

"How the hell do you expect me to get a job?" I retaliate as she ploughs through with her lecture.

"Eric Morrison, you are thirty-three years old next month. You have been famous, you have seen things that I will never get to see, and you have been places I will never get to go. If you, who has had everything, can't work it out, then who can? Who can?"

She has a habit of putting things in a way that you know, much to my annoyance, make sense. So I give in to her and set up an interview with a music recruitment agency.

You had to be in the industry to know this agency, for they never advertise and they aren't in the phone book. It's like all the best jobs; you have to know someone to get in the door.

It's a matter of weeks until Christmas and I am in the West End of London on Friday morning. The streets are so packed that I can't move any quicker than half an inch at a time. Finally, I open the doors above an overpriced clothes boutique. I enter with the view that I am going to be honest from the start about who I am.

I am greeted by a woman who doesn't make eye contact with anyone and I guess that even if I shove my fingers into the corners of her mouth and lift them up to make her smile, she would somehow still manage to frown at me.

"Please, hear me out," I plea as I'm told that the person who booked me in didn't realise who I was and me being Eric Morrison is a big problem.

"I was never charged. I was a great producer. I never did any of it." I get the look. The "you're as guilty as hell, you bastard" look.

"Well, why do you need me to get back into producing?" she asks, not even able to look into my corner of the room.

"Surely you must still have contacts?" she asks.

"Not anymore. Besides, I want to work in music, but behind the scenes; way behind. I was hoping to get more into the business side of it. I can't take fame, you see. It nearly drove me nuts. I should never have released singles under my own name."

"I really can't see how I can help you."

"Please look at my CV. I would be a great asset to your company." She isn't listening to me.

"We don't find work for producers and all the other jobs you need a degree for. Do you have a degree, Mr. Morrison?"

"You know I don't. Surely there must be something I can do?" I squirm.

"Well, let me go and speak to someone," she says, yawning. "But you have to admit that your situation isn't an easy one. There is a lot at stake. It isn't exactly textbook, now, is it?" She hyphenates textbook with her finger, aware that I'm only being nice to her to get a job.

"All I am asking for is another chance," I reply as I began to shift from side to side. I'm dying to take a piss, but I daren't ask as she is already annoyed with me taking up her time. Maybe I can hold it a little longer.

"Wait here why I go and speak to my partner." I resist the temptation to follow her arse with my eyes. I wouldn't do it with that stuck-up cow if my life depended on it. A couple of years ago she would have been the one falling at my feet! She would have had her head up my backside instead of mine up hers. I was A-list—I had a lifestyle that most men could only dream about. Oh, how the mighty have fallen, you might say, but from A-list to Z-list, what gives her the right to make me feel like nothing more than a piece of crap?

My Armani shoes have a scuff across the right toe. I doubt it can be repaired. Ironic, isn't it, that the day I got these shoes I believed that I had finally made it; then I ruined then on the day I became a nobody again. I hate these shoes, but apart from a few pairs of retro trainers they are the only decent pair I own.

Little Miss Anger trots back in; the bitch has only kept me there 30 minutes. She smells of cheese and onion sandwiches and judging by her face I guessed she has spent half an hour of my valuable time, "tarting her face up like a slapper." My words jump out before I can stop them.

"Mr. Morrison, you have just proven to me why we should not consider helping you."

"What are you talking about? You already made your decision the second you saw."

"Mr. Morrison, please leave. Now."

"With pleasure, you talentless bitch."

"Well, at least I've got a job!" she snarls back. "You, Mr. Morrison, are unemployable!"

"That's true. If you can consider spending your day acting like a little weasel 'work,' then I guess you can say you have a job!"

"I will give you two minutes to get out before I call the police!"

As I make my way out I find that I can no longer walk and if I don't act soon, I will lose the last inch of dignity I still have. In the glass room, with my back to the reception, I relieve myself into a large spider plant. The relief is instant and I don't really care if I get caught. When I am finished I sneak down the fire stairs.

On the way home I stop off at Janie's Oven for a bacon sandwich.

"Where is Janie?" I ask as timid Grace comes to take my order.

"She is sunning herself in the Algarve," she replies.

"Good for her!" I say and Grace smiles back at me nervously before going off to deal with a delivery. I'm kind of pleased, as I'm not in the mood to force conversation with someone who doesn't like talking much. Anyway, if the girl doesn't like talking, then why make her?

I have time to smoke a fag before she slaps a cup of coffee down in front of me. "Bacon sandwich will be a few more minutes, I'm afraid," she tells me, running off to flip an egg.

"I'm in no hurry."

"I wish the other customers could be as understanding," she mutters.

I dream into my coffee, demoralised by what happened earlier. This is the very reason why I didn't try it in the first place. That girl was five years my junior and yet she had the power to make me feel like the biggest loser that ever lived.

"Here you go!" Grace slaps my sandwich down, but I no longer want it. Out of politeness I force a tomato sauce-drenched mouthful painfully down my gullet.

"Do you want another coffee?"

"No thanks, I'm leaving now. Can you wrap the rest of my sandwich?"

Grace takes ages; it's not really her fault as four bikers and Barney from the off-Licence have come in for lunch.

I have changed my view of the world, for without a job I am a nobody, less then these guys standing next to me. When I was famous I wouldn't have dreamed of eating in a place like this ... too coarse I would have said, due to there being no such thing as a latte or espresso on the menu. I wouldn't have known the likes of Grace, Janie or Barnie as I would have thought that they were below me and believed that having a bit of money automatically meant I could push them around. I have been a bit of a wanker in my time.

I don't wait for my sandwich. Grace is in it up to her neck, besides beer is all I feel like.

So I trot off to The Lamb.

"Usual?" Sharon asks before I have even made it to the bar. The place is dead, full of old fossils and a couple of other losers like me. "Do They Know It's Christmas?" pumps out of the juke box. Cheap foil decorations drape over the smoke coloured paintwork.

I like it in here. It's not trendy or the sort of place that anyone from my old life would be seen dead in. I like that. There is no chance of running into anyone I wouldn't want to see. The friends I have in here haven't heard of Eric Morrison, the producer. Their music collection doesn't extend beyond 1985. If someone told them who I was, they would just laugh! To them I am Eric Morrison, the guy that keeps himself to himself and lives down the road. The guy that has time to drink during the day. The guy who doesn't cause too much trouble and who's biggest sin so far has being having to be carried outside one afternoon after downing eight pints on an empty stomach. The next day I went and bought Sharon a bottle of wine to apologise.

I am lucky today to get a comfortable chair. One of the old boys hasn't come in.

"Here, try these new beetroot and beef crisps," Sharon says.

"No thanks."

"That's what I thought until I tried the things." So I try one and she is right—they are OK.

The first mouthful of my pint is pure heaven. Images of past TV commercials where men dive into drinks with ice cubes and girls sip drinks on yachts and in decadent hotels, take me to taste paradise and back and keep me from the job section of my paper. It's great here, for no one cares what I am reading—Sharon probably thinks I'm ogling at some soft porn or football article when really I'm just happy to sit and stare into space as gormless and disinterested as I really am with things.

I can't take the fame shit, but there must be something I can do somewhere in the business where I can hide in an office and still have something to occupy my time. The woman at the agency didn't ever have any intention of giving me a chance. I am innocent and yet they treat me like a leper. I was never charged. I did make a mistake by becoming a little obsessive, but murder? Not me. Don't like blood. Don't like violence.

"Rachel, I love you," I whisper to myself.

"What was that, Eric?" Sharon asks, clearing my glass.

"Nothing … just talking to myself." I feel stupid, but she just laughs.

"You want to watch that, Eric; you might start answering yourself back!" She chuckles as her characteristic huge barmaid baps bounce and shine like butter. I watch for a second and return to my paper.

Sickness twisels around my head as my forehead secretes sweat. My own stomach punches me in the guts and just in the nick of time I make into the gents to vomit.

"You better take him home." I can hear Sharon outside the cubicle I am in.

"All right. Eric?" she asks.

"Just give me a moment."

"Yes, you better take him home. He was acting a little strange earlier. He's not drunk like last time, but I think he might have a fever."

"He's a grown man." I hear a man say.

"Please."

"Where does he live?"

"You know the Paradise hotel?"

"OK, but he can stick his head out the window."

With the help of Sharon's boyfriend and mate, I fall onto my bed. "Luisa. Luisa." I murmur as I lay in the cold light of day. I think I have missed her, or perhaps she has gone away.

It is dark when I come to. The sound of my window bashing in the wind shakes me awake. The window frame has seen better days—a bit like me, I guess.

It still perplexes me how the owners had the cheek to call the place a hotel. After all, aren't hotels supposed to be places that are a pleasure to stay at? The word "hotel" always sums up the image of fluffy white towels and miniature soaps and mini-bar drinks … oh, and pre-paid porn. Not that I'm into porn … fat-titted woman screaming the room down as some bent man shafts them over photocopiers. Perhaps it's because I've always been able to get anyone I've wanted to in the past that I find the whole idea of paying to watch two strangers doing it a turn off. In the past, whilst staying in a hotel, I've never been alone. And it's not as if I was ever on a mission to ensure I had flesh next to me each night—it just worked out like that until I met Rachel. Even now in my sad state of finance and older body I've still managed to pull Luisa. I am still a bit good-looking beneath my premature wrinkles, even if I now get my hair cut at a five pounds barber and my fitness regime consists of twenty-five push-ups and a hundred sit-ups a night, and that is only if the cockroaches stay away!

"Eric, what the hell are you doing in bed in the middle of the day?"

"Luisa! Luisa, I am sick."

"What? What happened? Did they agree to find you work and you are feeling sick at the prospect of having to do something for a change?"

"That's not fair! Smell my breath if you don't believe me. I can't help who I am—who I was."

"So tell me what happened."

"The usual shit. Please get me some water."

"Drink."

"Thanks. Basically, Luisa, I am fucked. They think I'm guilty."

"You need to study something new, Eric. You need to try something new."

"I have been trying to get something new, Luisa—and what good will it be for me to study now?"

"That's it—I'm going to go and see if I can get you a few shifts at the tapas bar. You're not Spanish, but perhaps they might consider you as they are short-staffed."

"It's not really my thing, Luisa."

"Neither is living off your poor, penniless girlfriend." She gives me one of those looks and I just lie there until I need to take a pee.

"Luisa, you smell good!" I say, returning from the bathroom with a fresher mouth.

"Eric, later we do it, now I have to go. Now remember to come down at the end of the night. Dress smart."

"But I'm sick."

"It's only for a bit, Eric, and besides, you are looking better already."

She is right, I am feeling better. The pains have gone, but I do feel weak.

I watch as she leaves and feel envious of her life. She has everything planned out. She might never be rich, but she has a plan in her head to get the best out of her life. In between her two jobs she studies chiropody. That's her grand plan; to one day open her own practice. "I am going to be a chiropodist to the stars, you know, Eric," she sometimes whispers at night as we lay together.

"I'm going to get my exams and be the most successful chiropodist ever."

I fear that if she grows tired of me and the great weight that I drag along, the weight of being convicted by tabloids, the weight that just gets bigger by the day, maybe if she does get sick of it I might not be able to see her again. There's something about Lusia that makes me feel alive. It's only when she is about that I see any chance of getting out of this negativity and forgetting Rachel once and for all.

The college prospectus that she so often pushes at me sits on the bed. Accountancy, American history, biology, dentistry, business studies, creative writing, pottery, dance workshop, car mechanic, counselling, theatre management, and a million more subjects can't intrigue me. I'm in my thirties, what the hell is Luisa thinking? As if I have time to start again. So I file it like I file all the other paperwork that she gives me and I drop it straight into the bin. What is Luisa thinking? Someone like me can't start again!

I am recovered from earlier and so I settle down for the worst part of the evening, the time between when Luisa goes to work and comes home. Maybe it was the bacon sandwich that pushed me over the edge? I can deal with the daytime, but the nighttime has traditionally been my favourite time of the day, but now it sucks. I've never understood why people stay in at this time—and for what? Some shit TV soap or ITV drama? I guess they have commitments, like the watering of plants or expensive babysitters to pay, or they might be missing the latest episode of *East Enders* or *Coronation Street*. Cocaine and champagne and selfish sex in bed with some beauty was the closest I ever came to staying in. Now I wish my life away. I moan as if I was seventy and I even drive myself around the bend with my constant complaining. I had a life—now I am getting excited because James Bond is about to start on ITV. It's one of the Roger Moore ones, not sure which one, but perhaps I'll finish off the pizza and the beer in the fridge. My stomach can take it as it's been through a lot worse. I'm shallow, all right. If I can't handle being on my own for a few hours, then how the hell do I expect to make a living? Feeling sorry for myself, as usual. I don't fancy the film anymore, so I play Crash Bandicoot on the old PlayStation I still have. Georg's son, Demetrius, pops in for a second and lets me borrow his new CDs for an hour or so. The boy is eight years younger them me and is surprisingly thin, despite having Georg as his father. He's also bright and is at the age when he thinks everything is cool, including me, for some bizarre reason. He is the only other person apart from Luisa and Georg that I know. There is some kid in the background that I have noticed with him lately. The kid eyes me strangely, but not like most people, and it's weird but I can't really tell what he is thinking. He's also the only person who has had the balls to admit that he thought I was guilty before he got to know me. He promises me that if he ever gets rich enough that he will buy a studio for both of us to produce music. I don't have the heart to tell him that I'm not interested. Well, by the time he does make it he will have forgotten about it. He's working as a cab driver at the moment, but he has the same glint in his eyes that I had and no doubt a secret plan up his sleeve. Sometimes I buy weed off him and join him for a smoke in his car

"OK, Demetrius?" I say as he slops onto my bed.

"Fine. How are you mate?"

"OK."

"This is Tim."

"Got you, Tim."

Tim nods, hovering like a fly.

"Can't stay long. We're going out."

"That's OK, I have plans myself." He hands me my grass.

"Don't pay me yet, Eric. I will only spend the cash when I am out. Give it to me tomorrow-like."

"Sure," I say, closing the door behind me. I feel sort of sad. I could handle his company.

At eleven thirty I head off to meet her, still wearing my crumpled suit. I am sick on the way and cram half a packet of chewing gum into my mouth to hide the smell.

"Eric!" Luisa exclaims as I walk up to the bar. "I've had a word about a job! If Cero likes you, he tells me that you can have a job helping in the bar and kitchen."

"Great!" I reply, too stoned to care that she has kept her promise. It's my own fault, really. I let slip one night that I once had a summer job as a waiter in my late teens. There is one thing about Luisa, she has a mind that remembers everything you tell her.

"So you are the English layabout that Luisa wants me to give a job to?" Cero asks me like he's the Godfather as we squash into his backroom in the restaurant. His hair is silver and his body is choking with gold. A brown slim cigar sits burning in the ash tray. He smiles gently at Luisa, who lingers behind. Then as if she has read his mind, she leaves us to it.

"I'm afraid I am—but I wouldn't blame you for not wanting to take me on."

"Why is that, my friend?"

"Because of the things they say about me."

"Yes, the things they say about you—we all know them now, don't we, Mr. Morrison. I guess they were all lies in the paper?"

"Not all of them were lies, but most of them were extremely distorted."

"Yes, your have the look of villain at heart, but not the glare of a killer. Luisa may only be a waitress, but she's hardworking and no one, but no one, not even the king of Spain himself, can deceive that girl. She has put her reputation on the line for you and that isn't something you should take lightly. I believe that something did go wrong that night and I believe that you, like most men, can have a temper, but you are not a murderer! You just don't have the passion in you. A contradiction, you might say, as isn't the instinct to destroy within all of us? However, you Mr. Morrison, simply want to be loved."

I'm bewildered. This conversation feels like something off a film set. Who is this guy? He is unreal, but I do sort of like him in a twisted sort of way. He reminds me a bit of Al Pacino mixed with my father. My father was a farmer until he died three years ago. He never lived to see my shame. I am pleased—I am glad.

"So how come you know all this?" I challenge.

"Luisa is an upfront girl—she told me."

Luisa has never discussed anything about my past with me. I am not sure if I believe him, but I guess it doesn't matter.

"I see, but don't you worry about taking on the likes of me? What will people say?"

"No, my staff are very loyal and besides, no one will know you are here—they wouldn't believe it! If they did find out and things did get out of hand, then I trust that you would leave anyway."

"Sure."

"Anyway, you are old news, Mr. Morrison, and there are plenty of new famous people for the press to persecute in you absence. Now let's get down to business—shall we say eight pounds per hour to start with? I'll start you off helping four hours a night at weekends and on Wednesday evenings (Spanish night), and then if you prove yourself I will take you on at full-time hours."

"Fine by me," I say, not really believing the conversation, or rather, the confession of faith that his man has just shown for me. I am intrigued to what Spanish night is since the whole place is Spanish! I don't ask.

"Oh, and I understand you are an Arsenal fan?" he adds. "My team, too!"

"Really?"

"You start the day after boxing day."

"You won't regret this!" Luisa shouts as we make our way to the door. This causes an eruption of laughter from Cero and his waiters; fortunately, I'm on the other side of the door.

"Why did you do that, Luisa? They are going to think that I am under the thumb!

"I know. I'm sorry."

"They are going to think that I'm a wimp and that I need you to do everything for me."

"You are going to need a bit more of a sense of humour than you've got at the moment if you want to survive in that place! Besides, I would say that this is a stroll in the park compared to the music business! So what if I did get you the job? He wouldn't have taken you on if he didn't like you!"

I think she knows she is wrong. She didn't mean it; she's just pleased that I have got a job. If only I hadn't been so mainstream, perhaps I could go back to producing without attracting the shit. If it was just down to sex or drugs, then maybe middle England might have forgiven me, just like they did with that TV guy who got caught getting his bottom spanked in a brothel by the press, or the Blue Peter presenter who openly took cocaine and who, after being sacked by the BBC, managed to bounce back bigger than he had been. Even a rapper was accused of having child porn and though, like myself, I think he was never charged, but whilst still carrying the stigma managed to bag himself a number one single. The only other group of people in the public eye to be treated like me are the MPs. Sex scandal in the press equals loss of job and career. What I did was wrong, but what the whole of the UK thinks I did is still a far cry from the truth. What I was accused of scared middle England big time. I am innocent, after all. There was no proof, but we live in a country where trial is by media. Once they have accused you of something, then it's down to the press to decide for the rest of country when or if they will ever forgive you. I stuck my fingers up to them on too many occasions; I was arrogant, but not in a loveable way. Rachel, on the other hand, played them like a piano and the tunes she chose made them weep like babies on the day her body and her two-year-old daughter's were found.

Preconceptions
December-January 2002

On my first night at Cero's Tapas I soon realise that this job just isn't going to be an easy ride. Cero expects me to work hard for my money, like the other staff. The other staff, however, see me as having an easy ride. They all speak English, but refuse to do so in front of my face. I have to learn Spanish, to darken my hair, and whilst serving, blend in with the rest of them. Luisa helps me with the Spanish the best she can, but like most British people, I am crap at it, but try to improve.

The others' pig-headedness is driving her mad inside, but she won't interfere, for this just makes them hate me more and they already hate me enough. If I had come into this restaurant when I was famous they would all have been bending over their stuck-up noses to kiss my arse. Now they want me to kiss theirs!

I want to quit, but their stubbornness only makes me more determined to stay. I turn up on-time and never moan or complain no matter how bad the task is that they are presenting me. I do everything right. It's not a hard job, there isn't that much to it; Luisa was right.

It seems like it should be a long, drawn-out process, like it should take months and months, but it doesn't, nothing as bad as that.

Eventually, after weeks of chaos, they start speaking to me again. It's only on work matters, though, and this is just because Cero overhears them taunting me in Spanish and lays into them. Luisa tells me Cero was bullied at school and won't tolerate it. But, hey, at least they are speaking, even if their words are prickly and the thorn of their sentences slice into my teeth.

"Hey, English! Get me tequila. Hey, English, where are my drinks?" It's back-breaking work when you're never given a break by anyone, but I just grin and bear it. My grin is perfect now; it pisses them off as the way I have perfected the precise turning up of my lips and the empty gaze that I simulate means they can't read me. They always like to know what makes me work. They have got no chance. No chance whatsoever.

The customers are also just as demanding. However, they are paying for good service, so I guess this is OK. They have the right to want the best, as I would. The other pricks I work with don't warrant the same service. I'm always the only one who is ever sent down to the cellar and I'm the one who always gets the blame if anything goes wrong. I'm the one they make clear up all the shit and who's never invited to join the others at the end of the night for a drink. I sit with them anyway, chipping in the few words of Spanish that I know—but no one listens.

"*Quiere repetir eso*? Could you say that again?"
No one does.
"*Mas despacio, por favour*. More slowly please."
They talk faster.
"*que desea, una cerveza*? What would you like—a beer?"
No one answers.

Luisa smiles across at me. She wants to sit next to me, but I have told her not to do so for her sake. I need them to accept me, not because I care, but only to show them that I have won. No, I do care a bit. I would like to be liked by at least one more person other than my girlfriend. I miss guy chats. Tough, really.

We reach the next level quickly as despite their games it does change eventually—but it's not as if I even do something deeply noble and selfless that makes them like me one day, like take a bullet for them or rescue one of their sons from a burning house. They just get bored of tormenting me and start on the new Romanian waiter. They gave me the harder time, though. Maybe it's nothing personal, but just part of their initiation. After all, I have bent over backward to make sure that nothing I do is annoying.

In the end they wave the white flag when they let me buy a round of drinks. Luisa doesn't smile across at me, she doesn't mention it to me, but the next night at the end of the evening she sits next to me and no one says a word.

Later, as she catches me watching her sleep and turns over in bed, I see a soft happy smile on her face.

Making it Big
December 2002

It's Wednesday morning and our day off before the rush of working the ridiculous Christmas and New Year's Eve shifts. We should both be relaxing. We have money coming in and next year we are going to get our own place. I want sex and cuddles and a day of pottering and Christmas shopping and late afternoon drinks at our local. Luisa, on the other hand, has got other ideas. She has been up for at least the last hour. She huffs and puffs as she battles to tidy our over-spilling room. A few weeks ago she moved in with me and gave up her room, much to fat Georg's protests. Much as I love her, she is pissing me off, as it has already been agreed, arranged, that today we weren't to do any sort of work and simply spend the day being together. After all, it is only usually one day a month that we ever get to spend the whole day and evening together without at least one of us having to go to work. Last night, Luisa announced that she was on so this has spoilt my plans for a good morning shag. I don't have the energy yet to let her know I am awake and that she is winding me up. I don't know why she feels the need to have to spill half my cupboard contents onto the floor and start sorting it. She has this funny idea of what is and what isn't rubbish.

"Why he keeps this stuff," she mumbles loud enough for me to hear. She is referring to my collection of "Hello!" magazines and the others containing articles about myself and, of course, Rachel.

BANG!

From the bottom of my dry hung-over lungs I have no choice then to grunt, "Please be quiet, Luisa—I am trying to sleep." I want to tape her tutting mouth shut. Zip her sound-making devices up like Zippy from Rainbow.

"Be quiet? This place is falling apart and you are asking me to be quiet?" She's in one of those, "Oh, I'm having to act like a martyr" moods. Still, from the smells that are drifting my way I'm not sure if she has got martyr confused with farter!

"Luisa, it's early. I have been working twelve-hour shifts all week, please, woman, chill." She won't listen to me. Women never listen to me, they just steal my cigarettes!

"You make out you are the only person who works! When am I expected to keep this place in order if I have to spend my life working and my spare time with my head in a book?"

"You're not expected to do anything. Besides, you've sat your exams, you don't need to study; you are qualified." She's not listening to me. She's in one of those moods.

"Eric, all you do is lay in that stinking bed. You know, I think you don't mind living like this."

"Today I don't, Luisa, you are right. Now, will you come back to bed? We are going to be moving, but not today. Please come back to bed. It's our day off, for fuck sake. I am so tired!"

"Just let me have a few minutes to clear this lot up."

"Luisa, leave it—bed! I promise I will sort it out later." I will just bin bag it all, then she can't moan anymore. Well, nothing fucking stops a woman, of course.

"I have a headache, Eric. You've given me one now."

"Have a bit more sleep and you will feel better. You need a rest. Please come back to bed."

"Eric, I am not a child."

"Why the hell are you acting like one?" I say so quiet that she doesn't hear me.

37

"I can't come back to bed with the place in a mess."

"Luisa, it doesn't matter what I say to you when you are in a mood like this; it will be nothing but wrong in your eyes."

"Shush, Morrison, you are right. We need some more sleep," she says, crawling in with me. She falls off at once. She should just listen to me. If she listens to me then we wouldn't have had this stupid argument. Girls!

I must have drifted off for a bit as the clock has moved around an hour since I last looked at it and that only seems moments ago! Cramp in my leg, caused by a pile of magazines restricting its movement, wakes me up. I slide them to the floor. They are stubborn at first, but once I get them to listen they realise that this is the only way to go. The last one falls open on Rachel (by fate?) and her rock-star boyfriend of the time. I try to ignore the page, but her photo keeps daring me to look at it and I have never been able to resist a good dare. So I look. I look at Rachel with her arm linked around her rock-star boyfriend, Mathew Waters. They are going into some West End premier. She is dressed casually, but still looks beautiful. Her black spider's web knitted dress that she made one weekend is stuck to her skin. Her tits covered strategically by a couple of crochet flowers. She acts as if she didn't know that the picture is being taken. She loved that kind of shit. However, like the issue, she is old news, she is no more. Still, I can't help feeling that through the power of the photograph she is somehow gloating at me.

"Eric, I always said you were a loser," she is saying, now that her pain has stopped, if she ever was in any sort of discomfort, of course. Mine, on the other hand, still comes and goes.

"What's the matter, sweetie?"

Luisa sounds happy. She rolls over in bed; her swollen bosoms stick to my arm. PMS can turn her into a mad woman one minute and little princess the next!

"Nothing," I say, scrunching and tossing the magazine into the bin. Every time I do this trick it hits the bin, but Rachel is with us now and she makes damn sure that it misses. She knows that Luisa is hot and easily aggravated .She wants to make sure that she spoils our day. Luisa jumps from the covers, the back of her pants are stained with blood. She is always doing this—I don't understand why she doesn't use something in bed. The magazine unwraps like candy in her hands.

"So, she still pisses you off, even now, Eric Morrison? Even in death she can still get to you, can't she?" Luisa's face has crease marks all over it from the ill-fitted sheets and her breath tastes stale.

"Shut up, Luisa."

"You are only annoyed because you can't hide anything from me."

"I'm not trying to hide anything from you, Luisa. I have told you before, I'm over her." She is ruining the day and if she expects me later to just snap out of it, then she can forget it!

"Then why are you shouting at me?"

"I am not shouting."

I wish she still had her own room today. It must add to her insult the fact I have a great big stonker as I clomp into the bathroom, slamming the door behind me. She wouldn't believe me if I turned around and said to her, "It's not because of Rachel, you know. Most men have one in the morning." I won't waste my breath, for if I start to justify myself to her she will only think that I have something to hide. I can't win, as usual.

"Open the door, Eric Morrison," she shouts under the door as I sit on the toilet. I carry on.

"So what am I to do with you, Eric Morrison? What am I to do?" I can't be bothered with her today.

"You tell me, Luisa!" I shout as nature is even acting stubborn and refusing to take its natural course. What's with this place?

"Don't blame me!" she screams.

Why the hell didn't I go straight to Eddy's party that night? If Eddy was there I would have slept at his and Rachel wouldn't have tagged along and I would have passed out in Eddy's spare room. Rachel and I would never have met. …

* 1997 Christmas Time

"So, Eric, are you coming back to mine?" Eddy asks as he plonks a cold bottle of beer into my hand. I like Eddy, he's my best mate.

"But you have just got drinks! What's the hurry to split?" I can barely walk, but I carry it off. I should still pull. I pull a lot. Eddy, on the other hand, looks like a motorbike courier with self-dreaded locks and a ginger goatee to match his hair. He is stocky in build and has Irish blue eyes.

"It doesn't matter. We can drink them on the way. I can hardly be the last one to turn up to my own party, now can I?"

I shrug.

He kind of has a point, but I don't want to go. Last time he did this to me I clung onto his leg, but he just flicked me out of his way.

"Eric, what's up? You were up for it earlier."

"I know, mate, but the place is just getting started."

"But you look pretty wrecked."

"I'm going to stay here." Eddy shrugged his shoulders at me as a girl with black hair and skin the colour of white paste surrounds us with about twenty others.

"Suit yourself, then. Ready?" he asks and the girl grins back at him. They follow him out the doors of the Brixton Academy. Despite his attitude I know him well and I can tell that he is dubious about leaving me alone. Every time he has, I have somehow managed to get in trouble. There was the picture of me and the Brazilian dancer scantily dressed at some seedy club that I ended up with in *The Sun* newspaper last month. Still, I am a grown man and he is right, he really shouldn't have to keep babysitting me all the time. He shouldn't feel responsible. I scan the room. I want sex and I want it tonight! I wouldn't get it at that party, that's for sure, as I know all of Eddy's girlfriends. A few of them are good-looking, but most of them are either rich crusties or vampy gothics in desperate need of some protein. There is nothing really there to keep me interested; besides, most of Eddy's parties involve some sort of drinking competition with some ropy tequila or leftover bottles of ouzo. Once we did Aftershock and the next morning was a shock as I found myself in bed with Frankenstein's bride!

I feel rough; I am turning from tipsy to feeling crap. Time to hit the gents.

Two hours later, I emerge. I have no account for how long I have spent in there.

"Shit, the party has died!" I say to a pretty brunette. Perhaps she will sleep with me. She might recognise me if I slip in who I am.

"Eddy told me to keep an eye on you, but I draw the line to invading the boy's bogs," a voice from behind me says.

"Who are you?" I ask as a blond, female version of Eddy stands with her hands resting on her boyish hips.

"I'm Jessica, if you are still coherent."

"Jessica? Jessica? Oh I know who you are. You're that student that Eddy would like to fuck." She ignores my comments. I guess she has heard worse and is likely to hear worse still as she climbs from the bottom of the career ladder.

"Yes, he asked me to keep an eye on you."

"Did he now, well."

"I'm here to see this next act and then I'll give you a lift home."

"You are so kind! But if you don't mind, Jessica, I'm going to sit this one out."

"I'll get you some water. Shit, Eric, you really can't hold your drinks, can you?"

I don't reply as I sink to the ground.

"The next girl is my friend's mate." A girl with black hair, who wasn't there before, lingers behind Jessica. I look over my shoulder to the pretty brunette, but some other guy is chatting her up.

"That should have been me!"

"She's great." The other girl speaks in a winey Bill & Ted voice.

"Really!" I reply, taking the girl off. Jessica just smiles at me. I suppose she is pissed off with Eddy for making her stay behind and watch me. That sly old dog.

"What's the singer called?" I ask.

"Rachel Garbo. She sounds like the singer out of the Corrs."

"A bit pretentious with the old name, isn't she?"

"I think it's her own name," the other girl adds.

I can't help goggling at both women. They both have lip piercings and I wonder how either of them manages to kiss or give head with all that metal shit in their faces! Still, this isn't something that I'm likely to have to worry about as Eddy told me that she isn't into men, only girls. She isn't really my sort anyway, even if I do have a boner! A bit too scruffy for my liking, but she does have great tits. The other girl is a dog.

The stage lights up and ends the chattering. My eyes whirl erratically around as I try to make out the girl. "I can't see her."

"We should shuffle forward," Jessica says. "Stay here if you want, Eric."

"But I can't see!" I shout

"Come with us, then!"

A girl steps onto the stage. She has a way about her that reminds me of a mixture of a brunette Marilyn Monroe and a shorter Catherine Zeta-Jones. She is squeezed into a red Lycra dress and her lips and nails are the colour of blood. Her face is pretty and her voice is in tune, but nothing like The Corrs. I clock all of this in the first thirty seconds. I have watched many musicians, some talented and some crap, but I can tell you I can always tell if they are going to make it. Rachel had something—even if she wasn't talented.

She sings about three songs; one of them is a Transvision Vamp cover.

I tried to keep awake, but I feel off.

"Well, that was hardly worth waiting for!" Jessica purrs

"No, I think the girl had something," I reply

"Yes, tits," the other girl adds.

"Yes, tits." I smile.

"Come on, Eric, I'll give you a lift home—I just have to make one stop off."

Both girls drag me off to the car.

Jessica drives to Eddy's, once outside she calls him to come and help. I stare out one window whilst the girl with no name just sits, sulking.

"He's coming now," Jessica tells the girl, who doesn't move her gaze from the window. Reaching into her glove box, Jessica retrieves a camera; she snaps me, smashed out of my face. My mouth won't move to tell her to go and fuck herself.

I later learned that the picture would come in handy, for after she has finished working with us and is in need of some extra income.

*Back to Now

"Eric, what the hell are you doing in there?" Luisa bangs on the door.

"Taking a crap"

"For forty minutes!"

"I suppose."

"Well, hurry up. I need to go."

"OK. Give me a minute!"

"No, come out now! I am going to be late for work!"

"There is no work. We have the day off!"

"I might work anyhow, for you have pissed me off."

"Breathing is enough to piss you off today, Luisa!"

I open the door in the end to watch Luisa making for the door; she is fully dressed and has a face that is sinking to the ground.

"Luisa, don't go. I need you, baby." I touch her shoulder, but she pushes it off.

"Stop shitting on me, Eric, for I won't take it, you know."

"I know, baby, get in the shower and I will take you out. I think we both need to relax."

House Guest

"Eric?" I can hear a woman's voice calling me; this is strange as I didn't bring anyone home with me last night. Eddy brought me home alone. He must have pulled, got his bird (maybe) to help get me out of his hair.

"Who is it?" I say, trying to see into the poor light of the living room. My eyes sting like two jelly fish. My irises are not corroborating with my attempt to make them focus, they just sting away as if they have all day to be in pain.

"When you are ready," I tell them, but they still take their time.

"Eric, don't be like that. Don't tell me that you don't remember." A slim silhouette comes into my sights. My blinds were very expensive, but are about as useful as an umbrella in a hurricane. The light is crap and distorted.

"Rachel," she replies, as fresh as gaspacho. "Don't say you don't remember me, Eric." Snow White stands in front of me and she is beautiful, with a face like a fairy princess. Somehow I get the impression that what lies beneath her exterior is not so pure and new.

"You're right, I don't. Anyway, how the hell did you get into my apartment?"

"You gave me a key," she says, waving it like bait in front of my nose. "You handed it to me last night before I got into the taxi."

"I gave you a key! I gave you a key!" I try to shout, but my mouth is too fucked. I reach to get my key back, but she quickly slips it into her pocket. I should snatch it off her.

"Yes, you told me to come back at three o'clock today to discuss me doing some vocals on that new DJ wonder single you're producing. I know I am half an hour early, but I would have thought a grown man, no matter how out of it he was last night, would be at least dressed at two thirty in the afternoon."

"Look, miss, I don't know how you got my key since I don't even know you! You are obviously some weirdo! Besides, why the hell would I give you my key the first time we met? Why would I do such a thing?"

"I don't know, but you bloody did!" She looks hot, sexy with temper. "Sorry to have wasted your time, Mr. Morrison. I don't suppose you remember that we had sex, either!" She walks away from me and I don't know why I'm listening to her. We never had sex; my new condom packet isn't opened.

"So where did you say we met?" I ask sarcastically, not buying this bitch at all.

"Last night, after the gig. I bumped into you at Eddy's party."

"But I didn't go to Eddy's party, I went home. His friend Jessica drove me."

"You came to the party, Eric! Not until late, but you came. Bloody hell, you really have pickled your brain! You shouldn't drink if you can't take it."

I look at her in total disbelief. I don't like the fact that half my evening has gone and if the girl isn't telling the truth, then how the hell did she end up with a key to my apartment? The sex thing is still a mystery. I have no recollection of her body and she looked to be the sort of woman who you would remember having sex with.

"Wait while I get dressed. Then we will talk." I say to her.

"Fine by me," she replies, plonking herself into a chair. Fifteen minutes later I emerge from the bathroom with the smell of bacon wafting up my nose. I surrender to it. Just like in those cartoons, I am attached to its scent.

"Right, Rachel, I have been thinking," I start my pre-planned speech, still captivated by the food.

"Breakfast?" she asks, as if she is my girlfriend, producing the smell's source, a fry-up somehow made from my empty, mould-lined fridge.

"Thinking is good for the brain," she smirks, lighting up one of my cigarettes.

"Indeed," I say, unable to resist a mouthful of sausage. It is good sausage, and I eat the rest of the plate.

"Now I don't know what shit I promised you," I say, licking the tomato sauce that has splashed onto my hand, "but to be honest, I really can't remember anything after leaving the academy. Whatever bullshit I told you to get you into bed, well, I'm sorry. I'm really sorry, but I can't remember seeing you play, either. So how about I give you my card and you can give me a call next time you are playing and I can come and listen," I say, handing her my finished breakfast things as if I expected her to put them in the dishwasher behind her. Her lips pinch together and she kicks the breakfast bar in temper. I still haven't thrown her out. Why? Maybe I should have put the plate and cutlery in the machine myself.

"Bullshit, Eric. You won't ever bother. Why would you? You have nothing to gain. I need this, Eric. I'm different."

"Well, Rachel, how about you leave me your number and a tape and if I like it, I'll call you."

"How about you listen to it right now?" she snarls and I'm frightened. I should call the police, but she is sexy even if she scares me a bit. I like women like this, if I am to be honest.

"Then will you go, Rachel? I want my key back!" I say, not sure if I really mean it. I don't really have much on today and she is very sexy, even if she does plan to kill me, or worse.

"I will go, Eric," she says, pressing play on the CD recorder. "Now, listen." Her stuff isn't that much different, really, to all the other music I have heard, but she keeps plugging in how she has written most of all her own songs apart from two Transvison Vamp covers. "Oh, and I also play the piano and guitar," she adds.

The last song is the best and with some work I could almost

imagine it in the shops. Still want to get her back for making me feel so intimidated, so I say to her, "So can you do all this live?"

"Didn't you see me the other night?"

"Pissed."

"I was that good, then."

She's annoyed with me. "Well, show me now."

"What?"

"If you are that good, then get up and sing for me now." So she does, taking it perfectly within her stride. She starts to play my guitar, well, and I start to wonder how to let her down. She can sing a bit, but the dancing is hopeless. She could make it, but I don't know why she thinks I'm going to help.

"So what do you think?" she asks, sitting on the edge of the sofa, her hands together like she's in prayer.

"I think it's good and … well … I'm going to show it to the other guys on Monday and see what they think."

"Really?" She beams. "You really liked my stuff?"

"Of course."

"Yessssss!" she screams as if she had just been told that she had got a record contract.

"Rachel, I can't promise anything. It is down to lots of things, but I will get them to take a look." She cuddles me.

"Do you want to have sex with me, Eric?" she says, dropping her clothes to the ground. She is wearing green underwear. Satin stuff that makes her breasts feel like green jelly in my hands. Her eyes are also green, but her hair is as black as the night. I don't remember her body as we move between sofa and floor for what feels like hours. I enjoy not being able to stop myself from falling under her spell. Rachel Garbo makes me gasp when I finally come. She is a siren and if you are lucky enough to have tasted her, I swear you will never be able to find anything as sweet.

She leaves shortly after and I secretly watch her from the blinds as she jumps onto the bus. It takes me ten minutes to remember that I have forgotten to re-claim my key.

Not Needed
Jan 1998-May 1998

The next evening after a Monday recording session from hell, I return home to find Rachel waiting for me. I just want to drop to my sofa, to order a takeaway, and to steal some time for myself, but instead I have to handle an attractive nutcase! January is going to be a busy month and I just don't need this today.

"Rachel," I say as she lies on my bed in a pink see-through baby doll, "we are not on a James Bond film set, you know. You don't even know me, but you think it is OK to steal a key to my apartment. What would my girlfriend have thought if she had been with me? I could call the police"

"Men like you never have girlfriends and if you want to go and call the old bill, go a head, call them! I am not stopping you, but you will look a complete idiot—you gave me the key."

"Just go, Rachel. I want some peace." She doesn't listen. I don't expect her to as she retaliates by sliding off the baby doll. The delicate fabric blows down the length of her body. Then, like an animal that is unable to control its instincts, I jump right in there, right into her domain. She climbs on top of me, her body writhing like an electric eel, and I come straightaway. I feel uncomfortable and I want to say something—anything—but don't. I feel an idiot.

She laughs as if she knew I would be a pushover.

Lighting a cigarette, we get into the covers. We don't speak and all the time the sensible side of me asks, *Eric, why are you doing this? You know you are going to regret it. That's twice, maybe three times, that you have had sex with this woman. Women like Rachel don't offer sex without wanting (expecting) a whole lot more in return.*

Then, as if by magic, and to prove my point, Rachel breaks the uncomfortable silence with a comment that is as direct as a homing missile. "So," she starts, "how you going to help me get a deal?"

"What? I don't own the record company, for fuck sake," I say, as my tiredness hits back.

"I do know that, Eric—I am not stupid, but you said you would play my tape to someone. Did you? If so, what did they say?"

"Rachel, all I could possibly do is maybe use you as a session singer and that, my dear, is hardly going to plunge you into superstardom."

"But you promised you would help."

"And I did—I took your tape down to the A and R office."

"That's not going to help; it's going to sit with all the rest gathering dust."

"Sometimes they listen; if they never listen to discs, then how would they ever get new acts? I'm afraid that you are just like all the other kids who want to make it in this dirty business." I am patronising, I know, but this girl thinks she is a ball breaker.

She doesn't answer, but snatches the joint back from me. Clocking something over, I guess.

"Pass me my nightdress," she says as if by wearing it she is going to gain some instant dignity.

She looks at me with a gaze full of a million starving kittens. Touching my hand, she finally says, "Eric, you can make it happen for me if you want to. You can pull rabbits out hats for me. I'm desperate. I will go mad if I don't make it. Please listen, I am begging you! We can be so great together and in return for your help, I will help you."

I smirk right back at her, carefully pulling my trousers on; driven with the need for water. Still, I have a feeling that nothing again is ever going to be able quash my thirst.

"So just how are you going to help me, Rachel?" I say, returning from the kitchen watered and now with Sprite, wine and an eclectic collection of takeaway menus. She laughs, taking the tray from me.

"You are getting a name, Eric—you are doing well, but if you really want to raise your profile into the levels of superstardom then you will need someone like me."

"I think I'm doing OK by myself," I laugh as only a second ago she was begging me to help her.

"Yes, you are doing *OK*, but as a partnership we could do better; we could be great—more than great—we could be the best! If you help me get a deal I will be make us the biggest celebrity couple that the world has ever seen. Look at Liz Hurley and Hugh Grant when they were together and Posh and Becks."

"But you're not even famous. Who's going to give a hoot about what you are doing?"

"*Yet*, Eric—I'm not even famous *yet*, but I will be a star—I just know I will."

How many times in my career had I heard that statement? Still, coming from Rachel it did seem more believable. "Maybe you will be famous, Rachel, maybe it will happen for you, but don't you know fame is a about luck and chances more than talent? It's about being in the right place at the right time, with the right music and the right look for the right market. You need all these things to be right to make it."

"That's how you are going to help me, Eric," she replied, drawing my mouth to hers. I should laugh at her naivety; and maybe shag her, then show her the door, but there is something more appealing about her than the other women who had tried to use me.

"Rachel, if you like, I can produce your demo; that way you might stand more of a chance."

"Thanks, Eric, that would be nice." Her teeth glean like snowflakes as she sweeps her tongue over the breadth of them.

Then before I know it, Rachel and I are going steady. Her lips are never far away from mine. She is a sweet, lingering smell; not unpleasant, but always there, impregnated to me like my eyes are to my head. Her scent, at times, mixes my stomach, making me feel mildly sick through too much consumption. Other times she tastes like chocolate fudge cake and even on the days when I have eaten too much—I still want more. God, I think she is a drug—a bad drug that you just don't want to be without.

We go to the right parties and with help, get her demo played. We get her a record deal. I even find myself producing the whole of her album. It does sound far-fetched, but it did work out to be that easy. She certainly gets her own way. She is good at promoting herself—the best I have seen. She has the guts of Madonna and the sheer bull determination of mountaineer.

It doesn't take long until her single is being hyped up by everyone. It gallops to the top of the charts. The next one does the same. With such fast success, Rachel's head swells with arrogance. I feel like I am running at ninety miles an hour and time is something that just runs away from me.

My own singles continue to sell well, but I am not so much of a brand as Rachel is. Anyway, who am I to argue with the rest and admit that despite her being my girlfriend, she is just like the rest of the wannabees with mediocre talent, great tits, and an obsession with fame? Do you think they care what I think? Was I as pretty as Rachel Garbo? Did I sell newspapers? Not as much without her, it seems. I am not jealous, for I plan to ask her to be my wife. Once the right time comes my way. Time, that bastard thing that jumps and pumps my days away.

After her album goes multi-platinum she sits opposite, grinning at me as bouquet after bouquet of flowers land on our doorstep. She knows I only helped her as I can't help myself in her company. Other birds who have (as I mentioned) implored similar tactics have always failed. Even I started out in my career mainly in between the legs of Jenny Rogers. Jenny Rogers, a delectable forty-year-old director whom had given me my first break in exchange for a rogering from a young man. She was sexy like the women out of *Sex in the City*, and her tits would rival any twenty-year-olds! Still, this wouldn't be the case forever and I'm sure she just used me to help her deal with the fact that her honey coloured skin would soon be stolen from her and replaced by lined sag.

Then, of course, there was Vanessa; she wasn't so long ago. Shortly after getting to number one in the album charts with Orange Men, I was on my way to a meeting at the record company for which I was running late. I had even broken out into a bit of a sweat. Then I got in the lift with Vanessa, a typical sort of good-looking girl that you find at a record company—blonde, with legs as long as giraffes. She did something in the advertising, even worked for Jenny until she left. I only knew her as I had seen her getting on my bus a few times. Only in London would I be getting the bus. Anyway, we are in the lift together and I'm finding it hard to hide the fact that I'm staring at her body. Suddenly, she walks up to me—up real close—I can feel her breath on my face. We stare at each other for a bit and just as I am about to ask her what is the problem, she pushes past and goes to the lift controls. She does something that makes it stop in-between floors.

"What's going on?" I say, but she says nothing and starts undoing her shirt. Underneath she isn't wearing a bra. I am really late now for my meeting as she takes my hands and places them on her breasts. They feel nice, but that's all that happens, for before I have time to really enjoy them she takes them away, does up her shirt and starts the lift up again. I am gob-smacked—the cheek of it!

She e-mails me later to say that if I want more I have to go and listen to her little brother sing at some pub. I reply to her, telling her to speak to the A and R department. The pub was miles away—way across the other side of the river, and anywhere that wasn't a straight tube or bus journey was more then I could be bothered with. She never replied. She already knew this. Still, I'm not totally a pig; I have had my fair share of shattered hearts, but when you get as big as I am you sort of lose all perspective of things; it's like the normal rules that apply to normal people are just for that—everyday rules for everyday people. I feel different as I don't need TV commercials and soap operas to tell me what to buy and religion to tell me what to think. The free thinkers such as me aren't governed anymore by these rules. Working in the music industry, I feel I have earned the right to be above any and everybody else. I work harder then most and there is more at stake for me then, say, the average city office slave. Well, I am only guessing, for I have never worked in an office. I just don't know why people follow this path. I can't think of anything more soul-destroying then punching numbers for a living.

The first time she makes it onto the front cover of the *Sun* newspaper, she seriously believes that she's a star. She is wearing a knitted see-through dress and she is linked on my arm, smoking a cigarette. Hardly the most stylish of outfit choices, but she's made it into the paper. She's number five in the album chart and after Jo Whiley raves about her on her Radio One—she's set to be the next big thing. It seems like the rest of the country is starting to take notice.

After this we hardly see each other. I have work coming out of my ears and she is so busy that in the past five months we have only touched base seven times. We meet up to see in the new year, just the two of us in our place. I am still going to ask her to marry me, but she can't stay the night, so I don't. After that, I can hardly ask her to marry me over the phone, now can I? Perhaps I can get some time off and surprise her one night—but there is little chance of this happening for a while. Still, that's the life we have chosen to live. It's only when Eddy catches me one day working out how many days it would be until I could see her again did I face up to the fact that I am starting to have a problem.

"Shit, Eric, you have got it bad, man. The girl is a hustler," he says, giving me one of his super-duper ready-rolled joints. The paper sticks to my lip as I suck at it.

"Don't you mean a whore?" I say, hoping he is going to quote me on this in front of Rachel.

"No, she's a hustler, and it seems that she has dripped you dry, man. She's taken all your spunk, all right. I don't suppose you have seen the latest *Now* magazine, have you?"

"No, why would I be reading that shit?"

Eddy scratched at his mane. "Shit, Eric, we have really lost you to her, haven't we? Why don't you forget the cow and go and fuck someone else for a change. There must be girls lining up for you, but you aren't interested, are you now? No, siree, you have taken a sniff of B.M.F.G."

"What?" I snap, wanting him to stop trying to talk in that strange way he has adopted lately.

"Blind mother fucker gas. Your woman is plastered all over that magazine with that guy out of the Orange Men. Apparently, they are engaged."

"Don't wind me up, Eddy. She was with me at New Year's."

"And she spent Valentine's with him!"

Five minutes later he returns with the magazine. "See! It's all true—she is dating Jason Waters."

She laughs at me out of the photo and I punch it out of Eddy's hand.

The engagement ring that I have been carrying in my pocket for so many months feels like a dead weight in my pocket, so I flush it down the toilet.

Girls are allowed to cry when they split up with someone. They are permitted to show their pain; to go on shopping sprees; eat big, fattening cakes; and have work colleagues take them to lunches or invite them to nights out. All to try and get you to forget. I, on the other hand, have to keep it together. I'm a man. I'm only in it to get laid. Love isn't something that is likely to happen to a man like me. I'm not going to be bought cakes.

Eddy had said from the start that he hated her. But even he knows that I had deadlines to make. Time is money and only band front men can have tantrums.

"Come on, lets get back to work," he says.

"Give me a minute"

I go into the toilets and cut some cocaine on the pissy toilet. Even that doesn't make me feel better. I've got a room full of damp-eared musicians eager for me to produce their first album as well as my own work to do. Oh, and the added humiliation of having to work with that bastard and the Orange Men's next album. I want to take my coat and run for the hills. But I can't as I am being paid a lot of money and a lot of money equals getting on with it.

After a difficult day, the album thankfully becomes a great success. It is dark and moody and the kids love it. I still wonder if it would have been this great if I had been happy. I shouted at the engineers so much that day that they end up just as miserable. The whole place had been miserable. I even think that Jonathan Red, the lead singer, cried at one point. His voice trembles at the end of the day as he thanks me for my time.

Straight to number one I go with my own single; it's a dancy number and Replica is a great vocalist. The dance world loves it; I beat everyone, every last fucking star; every British, French and American singer! I am king of the charts until Rachel comes along a week later and knocks me off my throne, dropping me down to number two.

Old Ghosts and Goblins
Summer 2003

The fact that Luisa is living in my room (much to Fat Georg's discomfort) means that it is cheaper to live in this money-scoffing city. However, it also means that there is nowhere for us to go to escape from each other, so when I get into one of my dark moods or she has PMS, our room becomes a buffing zone, a place for us to bang heads in! Regardless, I do enjoy living with her most of the time. I love her more than anything. Our love is real and not disguised as lust like it was with Rachel. No, this is the kind of love that beats at my heart so hard that I often wake sweating with the fear that it will end. With Rachel it was only my pride that was damaged with her rejection. I had a whole ton of pride back then, but it doesn't matter now, she is history.

I have never been a big romantic, but Lusia is everything to me. God, I am lucky in that sense, to find someone like Luisa and just because I was being a bum one day. Love doesn't always happen like this, as I am inclined to believe that generally there is no such thing as true love, because for most people there isn't. Marriage is nothing more then something programmed into us by the rest of society. The second we are bound together so often we seem to want to be free again. But what do these people think they are going to get elsewhere that they can't get at home? I think it takes someone strong to love another, to open up their minds to the possibility that life can have a meaning.

We are all, however, capable of lust; a sticky animal instinct that always ends in tears. Lust is dangerous, as I found out. It turns the receiver into a zombie driven by one purpose and one purpose alone … to make sure they get their hands on the person they are wanting. If this doesn't happen, then they will resort to anything. It is, after all, a game and one that must be won.

Last week I got promoted to assistant manager. Cero says that since I've started working here that the place has been packed every night! Looks like it's been decided for me, then … I am staying in this job. At least I have money now. Of course, I do get some royalties still, but I'm sticking them away for when I am old. They are not that great. I would though rather live with nothing now then piss it down the bog. I don't know how much I will have, but I won't touch it now. I have a cousin in Gibraltar who's holding it for me; not even Luisa knows this. I will tell her one day, surprise her, I guess, but if I tell her it sort of makes the money real and it can't be until I need it! My cousin has promised me that I can't have the bank book until I reach fifty, no matter how hard I want it. It won't be millions, maybe some hundreds of thousands, but I need to forget it. I nearly lost it all and I can't be trusted. I will just blow it in a month. I remember how to spend and where to spend it. If I get a sniff of that money I will not be able to stop myself. Even now I remember the smell of new leather car seats and that feeling you only get when you are driving a brand-new state-of-the-art automobile.

* * * * *

Late summer sweats about the place and gnats fly around the bed, the heat forces the window open and traffic noise into the room. They don't bite Luisa. She grew up in the countryside as a child. They don't like the taste of her anymore. They chew the shit out of me, though. Leave lots of red marks on my skin. Buzz like planes around my ears at night.

Luisa is snoring. She has a cold. I don't want to wake her. I have a can of beer on the side. I sit quietly drinking it as a couple of kids walk on the pavement across the road from me. They are dressed in jeans and walk as briskly as if it wasn't four in the morning. Their bedtime is near—where as mine has already ended. The girl flags a taxi that just happens to be passing and they are gone. The pavement is bare. Some cars pass, but it's nearly another hour before anyone else walks by. I cane five cigarettes in a row, flicking them out of the window as the ash tray is at the other side of the room. Some jogger in red shorts and matching T-shirt runs by. He's about forty and is getting a bit of a gut. I bet he went to the doctors' last year and they told him that he was overweight. Some big cat from the city, I guess. Too many work dinners. He has high blood pressure, I guess, and probably a drink problem. Lost his wife to some affair. Lives on his own now. Still, he lives in a nice place, but now eats rice cake sandwiches and has quit smoking, for if he didn't, then soon he would be dead. He has been doing this jogging thing for a while. You can tell by the rhythm he runs. He's white, so there is no way he has the rhythm naturally. He's learnt that. I bet his stomach is half the size it was. Still, he's got to lose more, keep off the drink. Prove to the kids that he isn't this womanizing piss head that their mother describes him as. Around the corner and then he is gone. Now a plumber or carpenter of some sort starting work early so he can get home early.

"Eric, aren't you tired?" Luisa mumbles, pulling my attention back to the room. Her hair is messy. She is sexy and I want her.

"Those gnats keep biting at me."

"They will get sick of you soon and go and bite someone else."

"I wish they would, for they are really pissing me off." She kisses me on the cheeks and I want her more.

"Eric, I have my exams today," she tells me, crawling out of my grip as I a prod her back.

"I know, at ten o'clock. You'll need a big meal in you, even if you don't want sex! Get in the shower and I'll take you for breakfast."

"No, I can't eat when I'm nervous … it makes me need to toilet.

Meet me later for a drink instead. I just need a bit of time by myself now."

"You can do it, Luisa; you are great at it," I say, but she's locked the bathroom door.

"I will do it, Eric, and then we can go back to my home."

"Yes, to your parents' little town near Seville."

"We can maybe get married," she says.

"Yes, and I could run a bar."

"We could have family."

"Your mother could help get you started. Maybe help with minor things."

"My mother would like that," she tells me, and I go off to work half an hour early so that she can have peace to compose herself.

Cero runs the place in a give-and-take way and today I'm giving, later I take. I have convinced him that he can get good lunchtime trade from the Business Design Centre and I've even introduced a new loyalty scheme, which means every fifteenth meal you get free. I hired a couple of promotions girls to go along the high street giving out leaflets. Cero is happy. It means he can go home for a few months and not have to worry about the place. He has left me in charge. The others lick my backside now, but I have earned their respect.

There is this great guy I heard playing at the piano bar, who is a singer. He's brilliant. I've got him playing on Saturday nights. The place loves it. *Time Out* also mentioned us last week. Things are going well. I've not been in a mood for a while and I've even persuaded Luisa to let her hair grow dark again instead of all that bleach. I feel a bit of a pig telling her how to have her hair, but that cheap colour always turns out brassy.

It's ten thirty and by now Luisa will be sitting her exams, scribbling away. I hope all the facts that she has programmed into her brain give her the answers.

"Hello, Eric." Margarita arrives. She's only eighteen and has a head of the wildest black curls I have ever seen. I think she should be going to college instead of dreaming of her boyfriend all day. She does make a good waitress, though. She's miles better then Luisa—

not that I would tell her so. She has a way with the customers. I like her.

Twelve o'clock comes and the early lunchtime rush is starting. Will Luisa be finished by now? She would ring. If she doesn't call soon, I will be too busy to speak to her.

One o'clock rolls around and I don't have time to breathe. There is a table of twenty just arrived, all expecting to be served quickly so that they can get back to work in time.

Two o'clock and I have sore feet and a plate of calamari rings and chips. Not on the menu, but prepared by Maria for a treat. Margarita brings me over a Coke. When I am finished I'm going to go and have a joint out the back. I suck the last bit of golden batter when a voice like the plague speaks to me.

"My God, it is you?"

"What?" I say, annoyed that someone is eating into the last five minutes of my break. I only get one break, after all, and I will be dammed if I don't take my full forty-five minutes!

"Eric Morrison! So this is where you have been hiding."

I look up. There is a medium-height man dressed in designer jeans and fitted T-shirt. He pushes his face right up to mine. So close I can see the spots on his face and, believe me, he's got a few! It's Mickey Waters, A and R executive, complete with ponytail and thinning nostrils. Mickey Waters, the guy I had once called a loser.

"Yes," I say, trying to keep cool. I guess he must have seen me serving outside and has come into gloat.

"Mickey?" I pretend to suddenly match his face.

"You bet," he says, punching me in the stomach. He winds me but I simply smile.

"What are you doing here?"

"My girlfriend lives in the new flats by Waterstones."

"Right," I say, conscious of the couple on table five needing their first course.

"Eric … you work here?" he asks as I take my plate into the kitchen.

"No, I run the place," I shout, bringing table five's food on my return.

"Why are you working here?" he asks, whistling to Margarita to come over a serve him.

"What you after?" I ask as I eye Margarita away.

"No mate, I'll get one of your monkeys to do it."

The guy still has the class of an unused bin liner.

"No, I'll get it, its part of my job," I say, wanting Micky to leave permanently.

"I want a bottle of champagne to go."

"But you have only just got here."

"Yes, but I'm feeling lucky today!" he says as a beautiful blonde stands smiling from the doorway."

I bet you are, I think. The girl must be blind to go out with a wanker like him.

"Here we're having a party on Wednesday night, if you fancy coming to it."

"Maybe," I say, with no intention of taking up his offer and desperately wanting to have my smoke.

"I'll be seeing you around then, Eric." He laughs. I half-expect him to say nice piny, but he doesn't. Shame, for I hardly need an excuse to smack him in the mouth and shatter his teeth like piano keys.

Later that night as I get home, Luisa is already waiting for me. She is wearing a green face mask and has a towel wrapped around her hair.

"Hello, Eric," she says,

"How did it go?" I say, approaching her for a kiss.

"Give me five minutes while I wash all this lot off and I'll tell you," she says.

I lie on the bed, wanting to shower, but as usual, Luisa takes more then fifteen minutes to come out.

"What you been doing?" I ask as she comes out in jeans.

"My hair." A canary mass of curls falls from beneath her head towel. Red marks scatter her scalp as she bends down to show me.

"Luisa, it's awful!" I gasp. "You were looking nice, why did you go and colour it?"

"I hate brown, it is boring!"

"Give it a chance; you have only just changed it!" She glares at me.

"Aren't you going to ask me how my exam went or don't you care, does my appearance only matter?" She's in one of those moods, I can tell.

"I do care—I just don't like your hair. You look more yellow then blonde."

"Eric, I'm not finished. I have to bleach it first, then put the colour on." She preens, snuggling up to me, and I pat at her head. The smell is bad, but I don't say so as I don't want to sound like one of those possessive boyfriends.

"So how do you think you did?" I ask.

"Pretty good, Eric," she says, twisting her arm around me.

"Luisa, I think you probably have done very well. In fact, I wouldn't be surprised if you got a first! And you know what that means, don't you?"

"This time next year we can move to Spain!"

"Luisa, things are looking up."

"I need to pass first!"

"You will. You know you will."

That evening I treat Luisa to a spot of food at the new Turkish place that has just opened around the corner. They've even got a garden. We would sit in the garden, but it's stormy today and too cold.

"Kebab good?" I ask, but Luisa just nods back at me. "My moussaka is nice"

"Can I try some?"

"Yes, but let me feed it to you."

"OK—yes, very nice."

"Fancy bumping into you again!"

"Mickey?" I say as Mickey and the posh bird stand beside us.

Luisa smiles between mouthfuls of meat. Her scalp is still red, though she has toned down the brashness. But from where they are standing they must be able to see. I like the red dress that she is wearing, but she has spilt red wine down it. Mickey's bird is dressed from head to toe in Joseph. Her hair is coloured like sand and her makeup perfect. I'm not saying that Luisa looks a dog, I think Luisa is beautiful, but on her budget there is no way she can begin to compete.

"Eric! I thought it was you! Didn't I say so, Easter, that I thought it was him?"

Easter nods with agreement and I feel like pinching Luisa. She seems fascinated with Easter. The Cartier watch, the pink fingernails, the elegance as the waiter passes her a menu. Mickey doesn't ask if we mind him joining us. Easter eyes the plates and I know what she is thinking. Well, maybe I am just speculating, but I reckon that before she started dating Mickey she would never have eaten in a place like this. But the place got a good review in *Time Out* and, after all, isn't it something to tell mummy about or even bring her to next time she comes to stay. She wants to show how independent and street wise her precious little Easter has become. Even if she did let mummy pay the deposit on her half-a-million flat, then kindly got Heals Outfitters to kit it out for her. She is probably a nice girl, but I have to admit that I am kind of prejudiced against rich kids—they annoy me that way they cruise through life without a clue about what is going on. I'm not even hard-core working class. I had a reasonable childhood, but the way the rich swan around this town like they own the place really pisses me off! I just can't see the point of having them other than to annoy.

"So, Luisa, what do you do for a living?" Mickey digs.

"Waitressing at the moment," she chews at him. "But by this time next year I'm going to be a qualified chiropodist, then Eric and I are going to move to Spain."

"And what's Eric going to do whilst you're corn doctoring?" He smirks.

"Re-open my mother's restaurant," Luisa snaps.

Mickey laughs. How the hell did he get a bird like Easter? I had to know.

"So, Easter, where did you two meet?" I ask, trying to stop my forehead from sweating. I don't know how I expect to suddenly gain this ability. I can't, but Mickey knows he is making me sweat and he is loving every minute of it.

"Oh, I did the PR for a gig at *Popcorn*." She smiles awkwardly. "We met there."

"I see," I say, as my voice and mannerisms snap back into their old ways. There is no way he is going to make me feel like shit! I wink at Easter in that way the girls seem to like. Luisa is too busy staring at Mickey to notice. Really it's not what I said back then but just the way I said it. It's difficult to understand, to describe—it's all down to tone of voice really.

"Want a drink?" I ask,

"Why, are you buying?" Easter purrs.

"What ever you want, baby." Luisa kicks me under the table, but I don't mean any of it. Easter smiles like a cat back at me and in the old days I wouldn't have cared about dumping Luisa. Nowadays, of course, this is different and anyway Easter doesn't mean it either, she's just using me to remind Mickey that he is lucky to have her.

Mickey butts in, and I know I have wound him up. "Really, Eric, there is no need to look sad; I'm sure someone must have something you can do other than scrub plates! I have an office junior position that you can have!"

Luisa is losing it. I can tell she is losing her temper as her nose is twitching.

"Don't be so rude to him! He runs a restaurant! I'd like to see you do so. Stop taking the piss and showing off in front of your posh lady friend, for believe me, from where I'm sitting I can see that she is far from impressed!" Luisa doesn't take a breath.

"Well, you, my darling, should learn to shut up. I mean, Eric, can't you keep your dog on a lead? If she's not careful, she might trip over that bottom lip of hers." Luisa has now been pushed well over her limit of respect and calmness. Like a Rottweiler she goes straight for where it hurts.

"Well, Mickey, at least Eric doesn't have to pay for some high-society call girl; at least he can get a woman on his own merit! Now we were enjoying our meal until you turned up, so do us both a favour and go and get lost."

"Yes, get lost, Mickey; I think it's best that you don't join us. We were kind of making a night of it." I add, backing up my woman.

Calmly, Luisa caries on eating. Easter just stares at her. "Waiter, would you mind getting us some more drinks. The same again please," Luisa asks

"I don't think I could bear another second with any of you." And with that, Easter rises like a princess and floats into the street.

"Now look what you have done, you slag." Mickey stamps his fist on the table, causing a waiter to come over. "What happened to you, Eric? How did you become such a loser?"

"Everything all right?" the waiter asks, grabbing onto Mickey's arm.

"Yes, Mickey was just leaving, weren't you? Now get lost," I say, proud of Luisa.

"Don't worry, Eric, I'm going, but you haven't heard the last of me."

"Whatever!" I say as he is shown out.

"Luisa, you are crazy," I say, kissing her on the forehead.

"Well, I think you should ask me to marry you," she says, turning pink, but I don't reply and she acts like the words never jumped out in the way they just did. Still I have to admit that a Spanish wedding in the sun and Luisa decked in catholic lace does jump into my mind. The simple life, with lots of children, could this really be my destiny? Me, Eric, who was once almost the greatest producer in Britain, could I settle for the simplistic and for contentment?

"Luisa, I think we should both have a coffee." I say, feeling bouts of panic and the smell of shitty nappies stinking into my imagination.

"Maybe, Eric, I do like coffee … don't worry, Eric, pricks like that are all bark and no bite as you say."

"Believe me, that guy's got just as much bite as he has bark," I say, knowing full-well that it's all just a matter of time before he finds some way to fuck me over.

"Luisa, shall we get the bill? I feel like having you all to myself." She giggles back at me.

Machete
August 2003

"Eric! Eric, you have to wake up. For fuck sake, Eric, are you pissed or what? Wake up!" A man's voice, young and full of bad pronunciation, runs into my ears.

I am, in fact, awake, but until I work out whom the hell it is trespassing in my room on what has been a mega-bad night, I am keeping put.

"It is no good, he is dead to the world," Luisa tells them.

"But we need him, man, he has to help us," a different voice in the same slang speaks.

"Maybe it will be OK—Georg might understand," she offers and though I have my eyes closed I guess they are looking at her as if she is crazy, for I know that when it comes to Fat Georg and his son, it is something he takes very seriously, however it may appear to anyone else.

"Are you crazy? It was only last week that Georg threatened him with sending him back, back to Greece if he so much as sneezed out of place again and this was just for a speeding fine and some unpaid parking tickets. How do you think he will react if he knew that he was now lying unconscious, feet from his own vomit, in a room that is to be used for his niece's christening party tomorrow?"

67

Luisa doesn't say a word and the boy continues on, his voice almost reaching a squeak as he hurries to convey his story. "You think that Fat Georg will understand that he has taken too much acid and that every time we go near him to move him he waves a machete at our face as he thinks we are trying to kill him?"

"I just don't know. I just don't know what to say. I am supposed to clean the place at six a.m., which is only two hours away, and I'll be dammed if I'm going to lose my job over it and if you don't get out of here and let me get some sleep I am not going to be in a fit state for anything tomorrow."

"Luisa, don't worry, I'm awake. I'm going," I say, falling into my jeans. The two boys look like a cross between Ali G. and Kevin the Teenager as I push them out the way. They are so bling-bling that they make Jimmy Saville look like an introvert. One of the guys I recognise as Tim, a boy that seems to be around this place all the time and probably mustn't have a home to go to, either that or he is dead and permanently haunting the place! The other kid is called S.D. He has dyed blond hair, the same cheap shit colour as Luisa, but even badder, and I guess he's trying to look a bit like Eminem. This doesn't work, though, as he is fat for his age and looks more like Fat Georg's son then Demetrius does. I don't know what the S.D. stands for, but it's easy enough to remember.

"I'm not surprised with the racket of these two. I just don't see why we need to get involved," she snaps.

"We don't know who else to ask," S.D. spits in a panic.

"I don't know how you think I can help," I add.

"He respects ya, man," they chorus.

"He will listen to you; besides, you have done loads of drugs … you'll know what to do," Tim says.

Luisa looks at me suspiciously and I want to steer them out of the room. That's all I need, more trouble. They make me sound like some junkie.

"A machete, you say?" I ask. Tim nods. "Shit, if he comes near me with that."

"Eric, we should call the police. I don't want you getting hurt," Luisa says.

"Luisa, we can't, it's just not an option. Now get some sleep—I shouldn't be long."

She tells me in Spanish that if I'm not back in twenty minutes she is going to call the old bill, but she won't do that. Georg would go spare if she did something like that without first consulting with him. "I mean it!" she burns her words out of the door.

I don't know why I have agreed to do this, for I don't feel like playing the big hero, but I like the kid and I guess he might do the same for me. Still, how the hell did he get his hands on a machete? Georg would send him to priest school if he knew half the stuff he got up to.

"Where's Fat Georg?" I ask as we reach the room.

"Asleep, of course." S.D. flicks his fingers like a rapper.

"I hope you are right. Have you checked his office?"

"He is! We checked! Anyhow, he's always bragging how nothing can wake him until he is ready," Tim sneers.

"Yeah, D is the same," S.D. says

"Right, a machete, you say?"

"Yes, oh, and there is another problem." S.D. avoids eye contact with me.

"What sort of problem?" The boys look at each other.

"He's sat on the cake."

"Cake?"

"Yes, the christening cake."

"I'm hardly a baker. What do you expect me to do, start baking?" I say, patronising, and S.D. laughs.

"Of course not," Tim snaps, "but you work in a restaurant."

"I'm a waiter."

"But the cake was handmade by his aunty."

"Let's concentrate on getting the knife off him first."

"Do you want us to come in with you?" S.D. asks.

"No, you keep look out down the corridor and, Tim, you watch me." Tim seems to like this, as he grins.

The door is open; well, it's hanging off the hinges as if it's taken a serious beating.

Demetrius is sprawled out on his back, directly on the floor. They forgot to tell me that he is naked from the waist down. I walk over to him, my feet creeping like ivy.

Demetrius looks like he is sleeping. This might be easier then I thought. Maybe I could still be tucked up in bed with Luisa, warming my body against hers instead of freezing my nuts off in the hallway, if these two stupid Herberts had just waited for him to pass out then simply taken the knife from him. Still, they are young and foolish, but hey, if he can't take his drugs then he shouldn't inflict the consequences on to others.

Before I want to, I have reached him … I watch as Demertruis's firm chest expands and deflates in time with his breathing. Not letting my eyes wander, I lower myself to the ground. The knife is loosely clenched in his right hand. I have to be quick for if I startle him, he might launch at me. So I go for it—as fast as I can I grab at the knife and get it. Tim sticks his thumb up at me from the door as I make like the wind out of the place.

"Shit!" Tim shouts at me. "Shit!"

"What?" I say, but before I have had a chance to do or say anything I am being tripped up in one of Demetruis's flash Kung Fu move. My legs fall over my head and I land in a crumpled way. The air has been bashed out of me and I can't move. It doesn't matter now, as it's too late by far, for he is kneeling over me with the knife beneath my neck and I am trapped. His cock is swinging in front of me and I am wondering with disappointment if this is going to be the image that I take to my grave. I think cocks are ugly, even if I have one myself, and the fact that there is one slapping only inches from my face is something to rightfully be worried about.

"You're not going to get away with it, you know," Demetrius spits. "I have my orders and you are not going to take over. They have picked me to stop it." He is looking through me. I am shitting my pants.

"I don't want to take over. It's me, Eric—I am here to help," I plea. "Your father is going to kill you unless we get this sorted out! Do you hear me! You will be picking olives for a living for the rest of your life!"

"They warned me that you would say something like this. They warned me that you would try and hypnotise me with your words."

"What?"

"You would tell a lie … they warned me about you. They did the same with the cat. Infected it. So I had to kill it."

"You killed your Dad's cat?"

"Skinned it—look over there if you don't believe me." Dragging me by the scruff of the neck he leads me to behind the chair. It is not a real cat. It is not Woody, it's a teddy bear (probably for the child tomorrow) ripped into nothing more then brown and off white bits of fluffy foam. I would laugh if I knew that I wasn't about to die.

"Demetrius, there are no aliens or whatever it is that your mind is making you think is there. No, you've just had too much acid. Now settle down, will you, for you are making a fool of yourself, and much as I like you I have to be honest and say that it's really starting to piss me off. I have been dragged from my bed in the middle of the night to help you before your father catches you and all you can do is parade around with you cock out."

"I am going to have to kill you—If I don't, the whole world will die."

"No one is going to die, Demetrius, you are just tripping. Do you want to go and live with your grandmother in the sticks where you're the only person there under the age of forty?"

He starts crying and lets go of me. I hate acid. I only did the stuff once and I hated it.

"I have to do this, you know!" he whines as saliva bands drool from the corners of his mouth and a stream of snot trickles toward his fat cupid's bow. I pat him on the back as he bows his head to the ground, but I am aware of the fact that he is still holding firmly onto the knife, so I make for the door. I don't have any choice; he will feel OK in a few hours.

"Stop it!" he screams and with the grace of a dart, the knife flies through the air. I duck in time as it misses my face by fractions. I can almost taste the bloodlike flavour of metal as it skims past me. This enrages me and I run straight up to Demetrius, punching him straight between his teeth. My punch is harder than I wanted it to be and the boy buckles to the ground. He spits a tooth from his mouth.

"Right, guys, tie him up," I shout at his friends standing behind me, frozen like overflavoured popsicles, not once trying to help.

"Why?" S.D. asks.

"We have to," Tim adds.

"Tie him up! I thought you were his mates—don't you know he is a black belt in Kung Fu? If he wakes up he could kill us all."

"Right, of course." SD moves to join Tim, who is already at Demetrius's body.

"Oh, and put his pants back on—I am not carrying a man without pants."

"What about the cake and the smashed-up room?"

"We will have to make it look like there has been a burglary. They will think it's one of the crack addicts from next door," I decide.

"Good plan," says Tim.

"S.D., you will have to stay with Demetrius tonight. Don't untie him until he wakes up. Tim, go and get some rubber gloves from the cleaning cupboard. We are going to have to turn this place over some more."

"Shit, are you sure it will work?" S.D. asks.

"It will work," Tim butts in, patting me on the back like I have just worked out the combination to a bank safe.

"Tim?"

"Yes."

"On your way out, fuck up the front lock like this is how they got in. It has to look real," I say.

"Sure," he says, "pleasure." He stares at me until I look away. Is he expecting something else, an even better idea that I don't have. "Oh, but I should take the TV as well … just to make it look real."

* * * * *

Luisa is sleeping by the time I get back. Her body is warm as I move her over from using the full width of the bed that she is hogging.

"Sorry," she says, waking, "I shouldn't have fallen asleep. You could have been hurt."

"Its fine, everything is fine. Go back to sleep."

The second she wakes she wants to know the score. "So, Eric, what happened, what happened?"

"Luisa, let me take a pee," I say, running to the toilet. She follows me in there. She should watch it as I am so tired that I could rip the head off a bear today.

"What happened, Eric?"

"Well, when the police arrive you have to act surprised."

"The police! What happened?"

"We had to make it look like there has been a burglary."

"What?"

"We had to, Luisa; don't look at me like that! Demetrius was out of it—he smashed the room."

"But the christening!"

"Exactly, and the cake is ruined. We had to do it this way, or Fat Georg will have Demetrius's guts for garters."

"Maybe he should. Eric, when did you learn to lie like this?"

"I've been a teenager myself, Luisa. He will be fine in a few years."

"Yes, but at whose expense?"

"You are being dramatic."

"Dramatic? He could have killed you, Eric!"

"Maybe, maybe, Luisa, but he didn't."

"But the baby won't have a cake, this is awful. I cannot lie."

"Well, don't lie, but it means we will have to move out and you will lose your cleaning job, you know as well as I do that Georg won't tolerate us going behind his back like that. Luisa, he will blame you the most, as he trusts you."

"This it not fair. I haven't done anything."

"Well, he doesn't need to know, does he?"

"I guess we are left with no other choice now. Eric, next time you say no. I mean it."

"There won't be a next time. D knows he has done wrong.

Besides, you know those Greeks, they have a great community life, they pull together. I can't see it taking too long for them to get something out the bag. Didn't you say that the christening isn't until two o'clock? That gives Georg plenty of time to sort something out."

"Well, he does have another function room in the basement. He doesn't like using it as it damages the floor."

"There you go."

"I'm not happy about this, though. Wait until I get my hands on Demetrius."

"Wait until I do!"

"You really don't need any more shit, Eric!"

"There won't be as I have had a word."

KNOCK, KNOCK

"Eric—it might be the old bill!" She panics and I know if it is she will confess everything like she does to the priest in church.

"Keep it together, Luisa. Wait here," I say, reluctantly opening up.

"Oh, it's you!" I gasp as D stands opposite me.

"I have come to apologise," he says. He looks like he has been to hell and back, even more so with the black eye I gave him last night. Maybe I should have been a boxer with the strength that I hit him. It was just the panic in me, the instinct to want to say alive.

"Come in if you like, but I warn you Luisa is serious pissed with you," I whisper.

"Yeah, I guessed as much. I better come though, just in case Dad's sniffing about."

"Demetrius, what came over you? Last night you were crazy."

"I can't remember any of it, not even taking it."

"Why the machete?" I asked.

"I don't know, I thought it would be a laugh to own one."

"I didn't find it very funny."

Luisa comes out from hiding in the toilet and strides like the woman robot out of the terminator movie straight up to Demetrius and angrily slaps him across his face.

He looks back at her, gob-smacked. A red mark stings across his cheek.

"Luisa, I am sorry," he says, rubbing his face.

"You could have killed Eric. You have been acting like a disgrace. It could have lost me my home and job all because of you. I still could, as I bet your dad is suspicious since I never turned up to clean the room this morning."

"No, I already told him that I told you not to bother. He agrees with me that there is little point, since the room is wrecked.

"You did cause us a lot of trouble, Demetrius. We don't fancy ending up on the streets," I add.

"I know. I'm idiot. But I can't remember any of it, you know, not one moment."

"What did your dad say?"

"He thinks like Eric said, that kids from the estate broke in. They even found the TV smashed up down the road."

"I won't be able to watch satellite now," I moan.

"Yes, you will, I've ordered a new one. I told Dad it's the least I can do for not waking up and hearing the kids break in!"

He laughs, but then frowns as Luisa raises her eyebrows. "Anyway, Eric, everything is under control. The old bill is still investigating, but they have more or less said that it's pointless for them to pursue the matter any further since there are no fingerprints or witnesses."

"Good job for you, Demetrius, for Eric wouldn't be taking any of the blame, that's for sure." Demetrius squirms like a lemon. I have to save him, but there is no need as Luisa has lost patience and is headed down the corridor to help Georg.

I look at Demetrius and he knows that he has outstayed his welcome.

"My aunt is having the christening at hers," he says, trying to lift the mood.

"Oh, Luisa said he had a spare room upstairs."

"Na, he never uses that room, it was my mother's."

"Well, D, you better keep your nose down today."

"Will do. Thanks, Eric, and sorry about being naked."

"Yeah, it wasn't pretty, D."

I spread out on the bed with the plan of catching up with some sleep before work. It has been a hard night. *Pop World* is on and Destiny's Child are singing. They are sexy and the perfect trio to sing me to my sleep.

I'm nearly there when:

KNOCK, KNOCK

"What now!" I shout, amazed at how the last twenty-four hours have reminded me of some dodgy fringe theatre play.

"Eric, it's me, Tim."

"Jesus, what now?" I say, swinging it open.

"Sorry, mate." Tim is still wearing the same clothes as last night. "I just need somewhere to crash."

"Can't you go home then?" I snap. "I have had enough trouble from you lot."

"Well, not really as my nan is over for dinner. My mum is already pissed off with me for not coming home and she will expect me to amuse Nan and believe me, man, she's like hard work. I've been up all night and I'm fucked."

"Like the rest of us, Tim," I say, but he looks like he is about to cry. I find this strange as he's never seemed a soft touch.

"OK, mate, crash here for a bit, you can have the chair. But only until Luisa comes back."

Plans
A Week Later

"Luisa, are you really serious about this?" I ask as we cuddle up after a particularly satisfying shag.

"Yes, I really think we should move to Spain. It's wonderful and the Seville hasn't been ruined by you British like other bits have. I really want to do it."

"We always talked about it, but I never knew how serious you were."

"I feel very serious, Eric."

"Then we should do it sooner rather than later."

"Soon enough, but we need money. We should wait another six months, then we will have plenty of money saved by then. We are going to need savings, Eric."

"We don't need much more; I would rather just go for it," I say, seeing this as a way to escape from Mickey and the dirt that he must be planning to throw. "I can get work there. We can take our time and slowly get you in your own practice and me with the restaurant. There is one thing that we are going to need, though, and that's a car—don't screw your face up, Luisa, it's true. It makes sense."

"How does it make sense, Eric? It's not making sense to me!"

"It makes sense, Luisa, as we can drive to Spain. It will be cheaper, more fun, and we will always have the security of being able to sell it once we get there if anything goes wrong."

"Maybe, Eric, but nothing fancy. We don't need a fancy car."

"No, we don't, but we do need something that is going to get us there and not break down. Leave it to me, babe."

"I'm not sure if that is wise."

"Trust … Luisa."

"Trust?" She laughs, knowing that really she has no other choice. That's the way it seems to go if you hang around me, choices are minimum. Mickey will be coming for my blood soon and I don't want to be here when he starts hunting.

"All right, Tim?" I say.

"Eric!" Tim nods.

"It's funny how we always bump into each other in this corridor, isn't it?" He looks away. My God, I hope he doesn't think I am coming onto him!

"Yeah, might have something to do with D's bedroom being on the same floor."

"Is it? I thought he lived in the flat with his dad still."

"Na, man, he moved along the corridor last week. Suits us fine as it means we can smoke. His room stinks of weed all the time, though. Your missus has been giving him a hard time about it. Tells us that if D doesn't hide the smell better, she will tell Fat Georg."

"Oh, Luisa is OK, Tim, she's just thinking of you; Georg will be mad if he finds out. Anyway, is D in?"

"Na, but he has given me the keys. Come in, man, he won't be long. What's up anyhow?"

"Oh, I just need a new car and I wondered if he knew where I could get a cheap one? Nothing stolen, of course." The potent smell of good quality weed scents the room.

"Shit, it smells even stronger in here; no wonder Luisa said something. If Georg comes in here he will do his nut! Smells good."

"I know, man. Got any ideas on how to take the stink away?"

"Joss sticks?"

"My girl got me some … don't work."

"Air freshener?"

"Tried it."

"Well, open the bloody window and smoke it out of that."

"Na, D doesn't want to in case the dealers next door see him."

"So."

"So?"

"So he hasn't bought anything off them for a while. Told them some shit about going on the straight and narrow. He's using another dealer who is cheaper and better. If they find out, we are all in shit. This is their territory. Besides, he owes one of them a favour. He's fucked if they find out."

"Have they got nothing better to do then spy at this place?" Tim shrugs his shoulders, but I ignore him. "Besides," I continue, "how are they going to know which one's his room?"

"I don't know, they just know."

Tim has dirty nails and he looks like he has been sleeping rough. Mind you, if he has been sleeping on D's floor, apart from it being warm, it's as good as. Luisa must be refusing to clean the place.

"He's a bit paranoid," Tim adds, watching me in a weird way again. I think he wants to ask me something.

Jumping to his feet as if he was just stung by a bee or something, he paces over to D's grey MFI draws. He rummages in the top one and pulls out a pipe; it looks like it's from India or somewhere Far East as it has carvings all over it and no one in the West would have the patience to make such a thing.

"What you doing?" I ask, worried that he's about to prepare crack or something.

"Never smoked weed through a pipe then?" he asks, sounding the older one.

"Always been a coke man myself."

"Nah, that stuff just makes you a tosser. Weed is what you want. Suck this."

I'm not sure why I have never smoked a pipe until now. When I was a teenager I was only interested in acid and E.

"Good?" Tim asks as if he is introducing me to drugs for the first time. "Ha, Eric, man, you crack me up." He chuckles.

"I don't know why as I am just thinking about how I managed to persuade Luisa that we really need a car."

"Yeah, how'd you do it?"

"Ah, mind games. Mind games," I say. "I managed to make her think that we need to drive to Spain."

"And Luisa bought it!"

"Yes, she bought it!"

"Silly bird."

"Women," I say. "Women, you can't live with them, nor live without 'em."

We have another one and I find myself sinking. I want to know more about this strange kid. This strange, ugly, smelly kid which reminds me of a mutt that you just don't have the heart to turn away.

"Tim, have you ever been in love?" I slip in, wondering what blind girl in their right mind would want to go anywhere near him.

"Na, not in love. Went steady for two months once with a girl called Annie. I kind of liked her."

"What went wrong?" I say, amazed that he actually pulled someone once.

"You know, once you fall for them they grab you by the balls then snap them off."

"Yeah, I know Tim, I have had the same thing happen, but thankfully Luisa isn't like that." He sneers at me as if to say I am an idiot to believe that a woman can be kind.

D comes into the room.

"Sorry I am late," he says. "I have just been upstairs having dinner."

"That's OK," Tim says.

"Eric, what you doing here?"

"I was wondering if you could sort me out a car. Nothing fancy, just something cheap and reliable."

"You been smoking, you two?" he says, sniffing the room.

"I just gave Eric a smoke of the pipe," Tim says.

"I see."

"Eric wants to buy a car."

"Yes … he has already said, Tim."

I can sense the tension between them, but I don't think it's just because of the dope; after all, I saved D's arse the other day so I hardly think he is going to begrudge me a smoke. There is something more to this. The anger in D seems to drip like a kid's snotty nose and though he is trying, he can't even hide it from me.

"I'm going, man," Tim finally says, averting his eyes from D's gaze. "I've got lots to do. I will leave you two to sort it out." And with that, Tim weasels out of the door. D has the lighter in his hand and wonder if it just crossed his mind to try and throw the thing at Tim like he did with the knife with me the other night.

"What's up with you two, man?" I ask D, who is now frowning.

"Oh, nothing, he just seems to live in my pocket at the moment."

"It sounded like you were expecting him."

"I was. I was going to tell him that he couldn't just come and go in the place like he has been; that my dad is getting pissed off. Some money went missing from the office last week and I am not saying it was him, but I'm not likely to be the one to steal it and neither is Dad, now, is he?"

"Sorry, man, I didn't know. Sounds serious. Maybe you should get a safe."

"That's the thing, we already have one and that is where the money was."

"Do you really think a kid like Tim has the intelligence to break into a safe? No insult intended. He is a nice boy, but I don't think he has the brain power."

"I suppose not," D says, scratching his head. "Anyway, we have ordered a new one, so hopefully it might work. It's just the principle, Eric. Just because we own this place doesn't mean we don't have the bills to pay."

D parts his curtains and stares out of the window. I guess he is watching Tim leave and feeling bad for being funny with his friend.

"Oh, by the way, I can pay you for the dope I smoked if that is a problem," I offer.

"There is no problem, Eric, I just wanted to have a quiet word with Tim. It doesn't matter anyway as I will see him tomorrow. You didn't know. It's not your fault."

He removes his coat and underneath he is dressed smartly, dressed like a well-dressed cab driver. He plonks a bag of money down on the side and then tips it into a tray and starts separating the notes, pounds and fifty pence into neat, precise money bags. His fingers have a few thick gold rings on and I can imagine if he doesn't get out of this business that he will end up with an open shirt, medallion and a round tubby stomach. At the moment he is handsome; well, Luisa says he is as I wouldn't know.

"I can come back if this is a bad time," I tell him.

"No, of course not, I owe you loads, Eric."

He seems to snap out of it, chucking me over a can of beer and picking up a pen and pad. "Go to this address tomorrow afternoon. It's my cousin's car place. I will call him in the morning and let him know that you are on your way."

"Thanks, D. D, don't look so down, it might not have been Tim that took the money."

"I know, he is your mate, but he doesn't have a job and his mother is an alcoholic. I don't want to believe it is him, I really don't, but I just don't know. Anyway, good luck at the car place and make sure he gives you a good deal."

"Thanks," I say, leaving him to his sadness. The corridors warp and twist a little as I make back to my room. That weed was strong.

"Where you been?" Luisa asks, sitting on the bed, painting her nails purple.

"D's cousin is going to do me a deal in the morning."

"Are you stoned, Eric Morrison?" she asks as I catch a glimpse of my glazed eyes in the mirror.

"Maybe a little," I say and she tuts as she finishes off her last little toe.

Visitor

With the excitement of getting the new car, a custard coloured second-hand Astra with more thousands of miles clocked on its clock then a millennium has years, I was thinking that somehow I was managing to forget Mickey. But I've just been sitting awkwardly in my own denial. I know it's all about to kick off again. After all, I have been happy for far too long now. Mickey wants to make me sweat.

He does make me sweat all right, I drip for a good three weeks before finally a *Mirror* freelance journalist swings his way through my doors near the end of a rigorous Saturday night shift. He is young and dressed in denim, but I can spot him a mile off. How could I miss that unforgiving look that I have so often received since the night they found her?

"Mr. Morrison, can I have a word?" he asks, flashing his ID at me. He's good-looking, but in a guy-at-the-office sort of way.

"I'll get you a drink on the house," I say, wondering if he will notice if I spit in it.

"Mike Miles, Mr. Morrison." He offers me his left hand. I pretend not to notice.

"Will you excuse me, sir, whilst I tend to the last of my customers?" Mike looks around; the place is deserted apart from one table of four, who are just leaving. Perhaps I should have thought of something else to say—like I'm feeling sick or that we don't serve people at this time of night.

"Mr. Morrison, you could put your side across."

"I was never charged, Mike, yet you and the rest of the press made sure you buried me into a deep hole."

"Maybe if you break your silence, you can put things right."

"Do I have any choice?"

"Not really, I need a story anyhow, so it's up to you how I get it!"

"Thought as much—wait here whilst I get rid of my staff. I'll lock up and then we can talk. But I expect you to listen to me from beginning to end."

"Oh, I will, Eric—all I want is a good story."

"And you will get it. I just want you to know that you have probably ruined my life again, for I will now have to leave my job and my girlfriend won't like it."

"Mr. Morrison, I have a contract for you to sign and it means that you will be given a hundred grand for this story—after this you won't need to work here—you can do what you want!"

"Give me a minute, I'm not sure what to do. Aren't my solicitors supposed to deal with this?"

"There's not time, besides, it's straight-forward."

I pull the blinds and take my place opposite Mike in the dim light.

"Just sign the contract, Eric. Formalities, I know, but something we need to get out of the way as we don't want things to get messy later—if you know what I mean."

"I know what you mean, all right—give me a pen."

"You won't regret this, Mr. Morrison."

"I think I will, but what can I do?"

"One thing, Mr. Morrison," he says, watching me sign after giving up on trying to read the unfathomable text of the contract, "how come you are talking to me now? How come you have decided to speak now after all this time? After all, all those made-up stories only occurred as a consequence of your stubbornness. I am not complaining, but you aren't exactly putting up one of your legendary fights."

"I guess I want the world to know the truth now."

"But why now, Eric?"

"Like you said, I have little choice." He writes frantically, in purposely unreadable style

"So how come you stopped working in the music industry?"

"Well, the truth is no one else would have me after they found Rachel and to be honest, the idea of fame and having to live within its confines was driving me crazy. Now are you ready, as I don't like repeating myself."

"I'm ready."

He smirks at me as I calmly flick a lighter and suck on the flame though my cigarette. It lights first off and the smoke is like the elixir of life to me, calming and making my head spin at the same time.

"Well, Mike, it sort of started when I met and feel in love with Rachel. She made it last long only because the rest of the country were fools."

"What?"

"Well, everyone saw Rachel as some sort of talent maverick. You stupid lot saw her as sweetness and light! You let her get away with things and blamed others for her mistakes like an overprotective mother, you spoilt her, spoilt her so much that she was only capable of demolishing others. She certainly destroyed me for a while."

"I wouldn't say we were that naïve, Mr. Morrison." He laughed, lighting up a cigarette. "But I do guess that we did take her side over yours, but you shouldn't take it to heart now as it was only because she wooed us. You, Eric, told us all where to go. You should know that it is us that make the decisions in this game and not you."

"Yes, even though I was the one that remained faithful, you still saw me as the villain."

"You were charged with supplying cocaine to a minor; even before the murder you had already pressed the self-destruct button."

"The cocaine thing was not my fault—you know the music industry—everyone is stuffing the shit up their nose. You can't give a party and having nothing for your guests. It was Eddy's bird; he liked them young, you see. She was just a student. She was a bit too young, but even he thought she was at least eighteen. How were we to know she wasn't even sixteen?"

"You had it bad, I agree, but you aren't perfectly innocent in all this."

"I never said I was! I am just saying what happened." I turn my body to the side. What is the point? He is going to crucify me in the papers.

"Getting back to the main point, Mr. Morrison." He knows I am about to walk. "Let's start from where things went wrong between Rachel and you."

"She used me," I snap. "We met at a party, or rather, she managed to get the key to my place and the next morning she practically demanded a record deal. She was always going on about what a brilliant team we made. Asked me to help her make it, so I did. I was used to casual sex with lots of woman—beautiful woman who knew I would offer them nothing in return. But Rachel was different, or so I thought. She was like a drug to me and when she started screwing around and decided that she didn't need or want me anymore, that I had fulfilled her purpose, as in got her introduced to the right crowd—I felt like my heart had been broken. I now know it was pride, but I vowed to take revenge, to never let her get away with what she had done. I wanted her to feel pain."

"So you hurt her?"

"No—I tried, but that was impossible. I couldn't hurt her. She could only hurt me. Like the day I learnt she was engaged to the guy out of the Orange Men. Eddy, my friend, also found out that she was two-timing with Ronnie Ederson."

"What, the owner of Planet Records?"

"Yes, at the time he was going though a nasty divorce settlement with his wife. His wife blamed his lack of fidelity for the split, you know, your paper wrote the stuff. He called her frigid and claimed that he had only ever been faithful. My plan was to expose them both and drag them down in the dirt where they both belonged! I wanted to do it in style, so I let my childhood fantasies take me away and I became a spy. I found a spy shop off Charing Cross road."

"You're taking the piss aren't you?" He laughs. "You, a spy!"

"No—listen. I still had the key to Rachel's first apartment. Ronnie could not risk being seen in a hotel and since Rachel no longer lived in the place it was the perfect venue to sneak away together."

"So how did Rachel's daughter come into all of this? Did you feel resentment toward her?"

"What, against a child that I have never met? Why would I?"

"I don't know."

"Rachel never even mentioned her daughter to me the whole time we were dating. I only found out she existed on the night that they found her! She was brought up in secret"

"Oh, that's right; she had her French mother looking after her in Lyon. She wasn't hiding her, Eric. She said she had her daughter's interests at heart."

"Maybe, but I know Rachel! Mike, shall I get us both a drink of something … all this talking is making me feel thirsty."

The truth is, I need a break. My whole body has turned to jelly and my insides feel like thy have gone through a mangle and back.

"We can call it a day if you like—I could meet you tomorrow morning."

"No, if it's all the same to you I would like to get it out of the way."

"OK, better make us some coffee. Can I have an Irish one? I can pay you, if you like."

"No, I'll make it."

I don't even have the sanctuary of a kitchen to escape into and compose my thoughts as the coffee machine is behind the bar and in full view of Mike. Mike goes to take a piss. I overfill the long coffee glasses with Jameson's, then coffee, mix in the brown sugar and drizzle the cream over the back of my spoon carefully. My coffees are the best and fill me with pride. My hand shakes as I dust over chocolate and chili powder; this gives it a bite. Going the full hog, I place two sugar-dusted Spanish biscuits onto the saucers.

I am a professional at whatever I do and I'm not going to let Mike think any different.

"Amazing! You make great coffee," he declares with icing sugar stuck to his lips. He has softened a little.

"The best in town!" I exclaim as my wrist continues to shake.

"So you say you pretended to be James Bond with the wish to entrap them both."

"Yes."

"Eric, this sounds like a movie script! I just don't understand why if you were doing OK, you didn't just forget her? After all, she wasn't your wife and she didn't want you, so why didn't you just get over it? You knew the game."

"I can't expect anyone to understand how she made me feel. It's impossible unless you have felt the same."

"But don't you have a girlfriend?"

"Yes, and I'm going to marry her."

"So it's the same thing as you had with Rachel?"

"No, not in your wildest dreams. Rachel was an obsession, she brought out a side in me that I never knew I had. It was a dark, evil side. I was addicted to her. I knew the whole time deep down that she was using me, but I didn't want to admit it. I know that in our business it is just a game, but she did stuff that made me believe we were going to be together for a while. I'm not gullible, Mike, but she had me convinced that she was genuine, but secretly I knew that she didn't care two hoots about me."

"So what would you do if your present girlfriend decided she didn't want you any more? How would you cope?"

"Badly, but that's just a risk I am going to take. That girl knows what she wants, so if she didn't want me anymore then you, me and the rest of the country would not be able to change her mind for her.

"Would you stalk her?"

"No! Have you been listening? Luisa is not the sort of woman to sleep around." Mike looks at me and I know I sound like a drip and when the paper comes out I'm going to sound like a total drip. I will have to spice it up a bit or all he will do is feed me to the dogs again.

"So tell me about you pretending to be James Bond," he asks, munching on my last biscuit.

"Eddy, my friend, made me go to one of his parties. I didn't have the energy to argue anymore. I just wasn't up for it, but Eddy couldn't believe the effect Rachel was having on me. I think it might not have been as bad if she had come out and dumped me, but I was being humiliated by *Heat* magazine and the papers. So later that night I go to one of Eddy's parties. I'm only there long enough to have a drink before a short-haired brunette with a face like Terri Hatcher comes over to me. We do a bit of small talk before she takes me upstairs. I screwed her in Eddy's shower cubicle, still fully dressed. Sounds good, doesn't it? But I wanted to stop. I hated every bit of it, even lost my erection. When I finished I found that I could barely smile at her. I was wicked, for I washed my hands and walked out of the house without so much as a goodbye, leaving the girl, no doubt, in tears. There is one thing to have a one night stand, but another to treat someone as if they are a prostitute.

"The next day I take a holiday. I lay low. Well, it's really a case of I decide halfway to work that I don't want to reach it. I can't face an ear bashing from Eric, so I don't go in. With a baseball cap and jeans I blended in with the rest of the out-of-work people who have nothing better to do than window shop on Tuesday morning. My single was at number one and I was hailed the new Fat Boy Slim. I was booked on to numerous talk shows and was starring on *Top of the Pops*, but now I wanted to blend in like tarmac.

"At about eleven, thirst dried my voice and I stopped at a coffee shop, tucked off Charing Cross road. I was sipping at an espresso when the shop opposite caught my eye.

"Samuel's Detective Gadgets was painted in red swirling paint. After my second cup and a line in the toilets, I make over to the window. The gadgets inside are amazing. Hidden cameras, voice recording instruments, etc. How was I to know that on entering the shop that it would lead to my destiny? The shop assistant must have thought that all his Christmas and birthdays must have come at once, for I bought lots of stuff—everything that he demonstrated to me, I bought.

"No one can find about this—can you guarantee this?" I asked as I handed him my card.

"Yes, sir, we are always discreet—it's our business to be. We hold no record of your name, I promise you this."

"So I spend fifty grand that day—just like that—just like it was fifty quid."

"But they were never exposed. I don't understand."

Mike looks at me as if I'm talking crap. I think he thinks my mind is so far gone from too many drugs.

"Listen, Mike, I can see from your expression that you are not buying this, but you have to listen and not make judgments until you know the whole truth. Like everything, there is a reason for this never coming to light. Perhaps another coffee?" Mike nods. This time I give him a triple Jameson and it seems to do the trick as he puts his feet up and stops looking at me as if I'm a bullshitter. I don't bullshit; I hate people thinking I do.

"Go on," Mike asks impatiently, clearly feeling the strain of the late hour.

"Rachel was ravishing as she showed Ronnie into her apartment. His wife would thank me for this, all right—I had told myself as I sat in the back of the transit like a sophisticated secret agent, thinking that what I was doing was for the good of mankind, when really I was acting like a kid with new toys and nothing else to do other than sit in a smelly van with a bottle of beer in one hand, my other switching between the controls. *How could you do this to me, Rachel?* I had shouted, *you are nothing more than cheap little whore with nothing more then a gift for manipulation.* I had talked for hours at the monitor, the camera was always zoomed on Rachel. Her eyes were heavily made up and judging by the way she was walking, she was wasted.

"Aren't you going to pour me a drink then?" She hummed, sliding onto the leather sofa.

"Sure," he said, as Rachel removed her dress. Her nipples filled my monitor and immediately I felt like a peeping Tom, so I zoomed out.

"The guy's dick was twitching in his pants and we were both captivated by Rachel in her pink knickers. Her breasts balanced perfectly on the coffee table as she leant over it to sniff a line.

"'What do you drink?' Ronnie asked, scratching his receding hairline.

"'Champagne,' she replied, not looking up at him. 'Actually, Ronnie, can you move that coffee table nearer—it will make it easier.'

"Ronnie was hardly the model of fitness and I had struggled to move the glass table. He didn't have a good body, but she didn't seem to care as she snorted at the table as if she wanted to consume the whole thing.

"'Can I have some of that? Watch it, Rachel,' he snapped, moving her head away from the table, but changed his mind and planted his little worm into her instead.

"I didn't kill her, Mike—I couldn't. I saw her right there for what she really was, nothing more than a cheap little slut who didn't mind selling any part of her body. I was over her, well on my way to being free. You see, we can't choose who and when someone is going to infatuate us, now can we? Nor for how long.

"They left after that. I had what I wanted, anyhow. I was going to sell that tape to everyone and was going to watch her drown.

"The following weekend I threw a party and that's when Eddy brought that young girl along—the one who got me done for giving her cocaine. She was the little sister to that girl I screwed in the shower and they were both out for revenge. Jesus, I never made her take it, but still she made sure she got me done for it. Then everyone came out of the wood work, anyone that could find a picture of me acting badly or remembered having sex with me spoke up."

"Still, Mr. Morrison, that was nothing, now was it, compared to what *did* happen."

"Yes, it did get pretty bad after that. I was drunk and stoned most nights after this and the more shit I put in myself the more I wanted. I was late all the time for work—that's if I even turned up and the press were geared toward a total character assignation of me, so I just couldn't escape. I was drowning, already finished.

"About a month later I decided to spy on Rachel again. I had been outside her flat for most of the day and was about to go home when she turned up late in the afternoon with a little redheaded child. The child kept calling her Mummy and I guessed who she was. It wasn't too hard to work out. They had played and watched TV together before shortly after seven. Rachel put the child to bed. She almost looked normal, like she was a caring, loving person. I had never seen her act like this, but, yes, she seemed a good mother, even if she must have hardly seen the child. Then at eight thirty he turned up. He had a black case and a face full of sweat. Rachel wore the Donna Karen dressing gown that I had bought her. It fell softly over her naked curves.

"'So, did they agree to promote me in America?' she asked as he scrunched fresh roses viciously into her hands. He wanted to cut her hands.

"'Rachel—it's all set up—you are going to be doing David Letterman next Thursday and lots of radio and TV shows.'

"She winked at him, but this guy was no fool.

"'No, you give me what I want, you little whore.' And opening his case he threw a black rubber Basque at her. 'Get into this.'

"Without question she did what he told her to do and began to undress him. Her daughter is asleep in the next room, unaware of the perversion occuring in the living room.

"'No!' he shouted, 'not me.'

"He fumbled with her a bit before blindfolding her and then chaining her to the fireplace.

"With a riding whip he hit her a few times and she begged him to stop—of course, with Rachel you didn't ever know if she was being serious. I wasn't concerned at this point, for this was standard S and M stuff. Not my bag, but not un-normal. Rachel wanted to fuck herself to the top and I wanted to make sure it was her downfall, or at the very least, like Mandy Smith, it would be the one thing she would have been remembered for. I figured when she got branded with the tarnished brush of 'Tart' that she would have to be content with being a celebrity rather then a star, and that I knew was the one place I could get at Rachel with.

"She hated celebrities, only stars were important to her. True, talented, worthwhile stars.

"Anyhow, he didn't fuck her at first but placed a scarf around her mouth so that she was now gagged. He got a knife out and lightly slit at her wrist. Just enough to cause a bit of blood. He sucked at her arm and the way Rachel was fidgeting I knew that she had had enough. He whipped her some more then picked up the fresh roses and whipped at her back. The thorns tore into her pale skin and he moaned with excitement as he grabbed her around the neck and started to have sex with her.

"I did feel sorry for her, but I couldn't help feeling that she might have brought it all on herself. How was I to know that when he had finished that she would crumple like a flower in his hands? He had strangled her to death. I'm not sure that was his intention, but he had done it all the same."

"So what did you do—you didn't call the police—why not?"

"I was going to call the police, but I remembered the little girl. So I rushed around there, but when I got around there the place was empty and the child was still sleeping, safe and like a little ginger angel. Ronnie had gone."

"So what did you do?"

"I ran."

"So that is why the next door neighbour saw you fleeing from the house?"

"Yes, but I panicked. I headed back to the van. The tapes would have the evidence and the shocking truth of what happened. The trouble is that in the meantime and in my panic I had left the keys in the engine and the door unlocked. Some bastard stole the van. I never found it. It might have even been Ronnie."

"What about DNA evidence? Couldn't you have gone to the police?"

"They would never have suspected him—only Eddy knew they were dating and he was killed in a car crash a few days later when a bus went into the back of him. I got a bit freaked out by it all, that fate was coming to get me, so I said nothing. How was I to know they couldn't find anything? Anyhow, Ronnie Edderson died the following week of a heart attack. He was cremated, so how could I have proved his involvement? Everyone I knew back then seemed to die. That is why I went into hiding, and have only now let myself get close to someone again."

"They found your spare key, though, didn't they?"

"Yes, but my fingerprints had been rubbed off by someone."

"I think that's enough Mr. Morrison."

"I agree," I say, just wanting to sleep.

"But I thank you; you are going to make me a rich man." Mike smiles and I watch him click the alarm of his Porsche and drive off into the faded night.

I sit there until dawn sunlight sprites into the room. I know that Luisa will be worried. What do I say to her? Well, after tomorrow, after this gets into print, things will change forever and she will never see me as just Eric Morrison.

Peace

"Luisa, time to get up, sweetie," I whisper, tenderly planting a kiss on her face.

"Is it really," she murmurs.

"I'm afraid so."

"But that is just so unfair."

"I know, but once you are up you will feel fine."

She rolls over, stretching her arms high over her head in a long, exaggerated stretch.

"You always tell me this, but I have never once found it to be the case!"

"Come, get yourself ready while I cook us some breakfast or you will be late for work. It's only for an hour or so, then we can have the day together."

"I'm going!" she says, making her way to the bathroom.

"Oh, by the way," I shout, "did you know that a whole lot of money went missing from the safe?" I try the bathroom door, but she has locked it.

"Yes, Georg said last night. He couldn't think how it happened as only him and Demetrius have the combination for it.

"D thinks it is Tim."

"Really?"

"Yes, but don't say anything. With things like that it's best not to get involved."

"I wouldn't dream of it," she says until her voice is drowned out by the noise of the shower.

The article presented itself as I waited for the kettle to boil. I pictured the brightly coloured front page of *The Mirror* and the headlines in bold ink, "I DIDN'T KILL HER," or "SHE WAS LIKE A DRUG THAT I HAD TO KEEP GOING BACK FOR."

As you can see, I am no journalist, but they will put some witty comment. They will show a picture of us together—maybe the one from the MTV awards where we are both dressed in chocolate brown. That's the best picture we ever had taken. They'll put something about it being an exclusive interview. The news is quiet this week so everyone will be interested. Maybe I should leave now and tell Luisa what happened last night and get a head start out of here before the paparazzi come for my blood. Women don't like men lying and if she finds out before I tell her—I'm dead. It's a case, though, of how to tell Luisa about all this. Where do I start? She might not like that fact that I have talked for money, or that I didn't come clean earlier. But if I do come clean, she might walk. Under the circumstances it might be best to wait for her reaction when the story goes to press and then try and talk my way out of it. Maybe she might see why I had to do it. When see sees how upset I am, she might soften. God, I don't know. Maybe it will be OK …

Even the archaic kettle has it in for me today; it just won't boil! I heat a king-size tin of Full Monty tinned breakfast for us to eat. I like to suck the skins off the beans and pile them up like shelled beetles. I don't like skin, be it that of a chicken, vegetable or fruit. This bugs Luisa sometimes as she is always left with the task of scraping my plate and to her that's a waste of food.

"Luisa!" I shout, banging on the bathroom door. "Come on, girl, breakfast is ready, you will be late!"

"I am coming! I am nearly done," she replies and I head back into the kitchen. I don't wait; she won't make it in time to eat. We both know this. The bean juice stings my ulcer, but I gulp the beans down anyway. I hate cold beans, so best to go at them when they are still piping hot.

I still feel hungry when I have finished, but I'm just being greedy. There is enough water in the kettle for my second cup of tea; if any bastard steals it I will go mad. I am always the one to fill up the kettle. Everyone else, even though I never see them, seems to empty it. *Clip clop...* some bastard is going to steal my water. It's not Luisa; she has her very own walk. She totters along erratically, her steps echo in either her little heeled boots or squeak in her off-white trainers. This walk is sloppy, but repetitive. I think I know who it belongs to.

"How's the car running?" Tim asks, drinking cold water straight from the tap. He wraps his lips around the spout, which is disgusting. Tim seems to have the knack of running into me whenever I'm not in the mood for chatting.

"It's going fine, mate, fine," I say, describing my cut-price Astra that D got me for £500. I was going to spend £800, but I blew the rest of the money on an engagement ring for Luisa. She's as pleased as punch and I can't believe she said yes. I'll get her something better when my cousin lets me have my cash. I don't tell Tim, he's a kid, he wouldn't understand; he would think I was soft or something.

"What have you done to your eye, Tim?" I ask, noticing how dirty his clothes look. In fact, they don't even look like the sort of clothes a boy of his age would choose to wear. They don't fit and resemble something out of a charity shop. Perhaps I am losing the plot— perhaps this is the fashion.

"It's nothing, don't worry." He looks away so as not to make eye contact with me. He always does that, as if I will somehow be able read his mind if his gaze accidentally meets mine. The soft side in me, though, feels a bit sorry for him even if I want to be alone.

"I better take Luisa her tea," I say. "She is like a bear with a sore head until she gets her caffeine. You can have her breakfast if you like. She isn't going to have time to eat it."

"Catch you later, then," Tim says lamely. "Don't want to piss your bird off now, do you?"

I hurry out of the room, feeling a bit of a bastard. The kid obviously had something he wanted to get off his chest. I bet it's about the money. If he has taken it, I don't want to know, as what would I say? Go to the police, put it back, leave the country?

"Luisa! Tea!" I shout, plonking it down on the bedside table, but she isn't there. A yellow Post-It note hangs precariously from our mirror.

"Georg needs a babysitter urgently for his nephew. Just at number six. Georg's sister is dead. Give it an hour then bring me breakfast. Luisa"

"Jesus, don't we ever get a quiet morning?" I slam the mirror. I don't know why I am so angry as it's hardly her fault; someone has died after all and it's not as if I would have said no. I'm just pissed off that yet again our day off has been ruined. She was only supposed to be cleaning for an hour to two, max—then we were going to go out. He better not expect her to clean as well after this. Georg will just have to understand that Luisa is not a slave and can't work every second of every day like everyone expects her to! It makes me mad.

Tim hasn't moved from the kitchen when I finally take the cup of cold tea to wash. His head is bowed between his hands.

"Rough night?" I ask, wanting to know what the fuck he has been doing.

He just nods—typical kid.

"Got in a fight or something?"

"If only things were that simple, Eric," he bleeps.

"Shit, Tim, what is? Having trouble at home? Have you done something you shouldn't have?" Reluctantly taking it down a road that might make him confess.

"Kind of," he coyly says and I'm annoyed; why doesn't he just say?

"Jesus, Tim. I can't help you if you don't give me a bit of a break!" I snap.

"Sorry, Eric." He starts to cry. "I'm just not used to anyone giving a shit. Can you just leave me as I'm crying like a poof and D's got enough on his plate with his aunt dying without having me bubbling everywhere."

"No one is here, you can cry all you like," I say, kicking the kitchen door shut.

"They think I am a thief!" He floods. "Me, steal from them! After all they have done for me."

"I'm sure they don't think that," I lie, hoping that Luisa will keep out of it and not mention D's fears to Georg. She isn't likely to, but I don't want Tim getting the blame until there is any proof.

"Try talking to them, Tim. That's all you can do. Tell them what you have told me. It will all be OK, you will see." He smiles at me and I wonder if this is what it is like to be a father.

"Thanks, mate," he says, as the colour returns to his face. "Maybe they will believe me."

"Do you want to talk about anything else?" I ask now that I am on a roll.

"No ... but thanks for the help. Eric, do you mind not telling the lads that I was crying?"

"Of course not. My lips are sealed."

"Well, you better go as Luisa will be passing out with hunger. I've been to his aunt's before and she never did have any food in her cupboards!"

"How do you know Luisa is there?" I ask, wondering if the kid has some special power or something.

"Oh, I saw her leave from the window with D—you must have just missed them."

"I must have."

By the time I get to the house it's almost lunchtime. The directions Tim gave me are pants. Her house is barely five minutes away, but he has sent me on the tour of North London route!

I've forgotten to ask the number. There are police everywhere and I remember what Tim said about D's aunt being dead and not really listening at the time.

"Over here!" Luisa shouts and she nods at a policeman to allow me into the house.

"Eric, I'm glad you are here," Luisa tells me softly as I step into the house.

"What happened?" I whisper.

"She was found strangled," She mouths. "Better be quiet as I have just managed to get her little girl to sleep."

"So why aren't the police in here? Surely they wouldn't let people just come and go?"

"Oh, she lived next door, this is Marion, her neighbour's house. They are over there now."

"Who killed her?"

"Some mugger, they think."

"Tim never mentioned she was murdered."

"Well, there are lots of rumours, so I guess everyone is keeping quiet. Marion, who lives here, has just called me to say that she will be back in two minutes—we can then go."

"Where is she, like?"

"Giving evidence. That is why Georg asked me to watch his niece."

I look at Luisa; her hair has dried funny and she has no makeup on. She is a beautiful girl, but this seems to be how she looks so often and I know it's nothing to do with neglect, she just doesn't get a second to herself.

"Do you ever get that feeling that we are living in the centre of a hurricane and that everything we touch just seems to get swept away?" I say as she washes and dries a black coffee cup.

"Today is different, Eric—someone is dead," she says, placing it onto the mug tree.

"Yes, but there is always something. I just would like to have a normal-ish day for once."

"I love you, Eric," Her words sound sincere.

"I love you, too, and when Marion gets back I am going to take you away from this madness for a bit. Just for the night. I am fed up with all this dirt and filth. We are going to stay in a hotel far away from all of this."

"But shouldn't we be saving for Spain?"

"Yes, but sometimes I think we have to do things just for the hell of it, if only to keep us sane. Now I will pop home and get an overnight bag and meet you at the bus stop in ten minutes."

"But how are we going to organise this? We haven't made any plans."

"There is no need. I will do it all. I remember my mate Eddy taking some bird to a nice hotel in Kent. We will go there. We can get the train and if it is full, there are plenty of others. Now don't argue."

No one looks at me as I step over the line.

I am running home.

I sprint to my room.

I don't care if anyone wants us—today is about me and Luisa and no one else is going to stop us having a good time.

I stuff everything we can both possibly need, my good old suit, Luisa's only nice dress, her makeup, underwear, tops, washing stuff, all into my posh brown bag. Then I run like the wind out of that door as fast as my legs can take me.

I think someone calls my name, or maybe I just imagine it, but either way I pretend I don't hear them. Today I can't help anyone; normally I would, but not today. Sometimes you just have to put yourself first.

*

"Fancy finding your mother dead," Luisa tells me over dinner at Brands Hatch Place hotel. We were lucky as the hotel had one cancellation that day and we have managed to get the bridal suite. This could be the last of the good times. The press could ruin it all again, so I want it to be a time to remember.

"Well, it's best we don't think about it," I say firmly, making it clear that the hotel or anyone associated with it isn't what we should be talking about tonight.

"Now do you want white or red wine?" She doesn't answer and I guess she can't switch off like that, so I order something special as she slips off to the loo.

By the time she gets back the waiter is serving us two big glasses of champagne.

"To us," I say.

"Eric, this is so bad."

"A bit like you in the sack."

"Eric!"

"Well, Luisa, we are here to have fun and not count the pennies for a change."

"I guess, Eric, you are right, you have brought me to this hotel and that's not likely to happen again. Well, at least not for a while. Eric Morrison, give me a kiss, a nice big kiss," she says as we finish our half bottle of champagne, and I can see she is tipsy already.

She looks beautiful tonight, I want her.

The waiter learns over us to pour the white wine that Luisa has chosen. It's some Spanish stuff. I prefer red, but perhaps it's not appropriate.

"That kid Tim came up to me when I was waiting at the bus stop for you," Luisa slips in.

"He seems to get everywhere," I say, pretending that she hasn't just ignored my request.

"I know, I think he should move into the hotel as he spends half his life there anyway."

"Did he speak to you much? He's a bit hard to get words out of sometimes."

"Only to say that you were a great bloke and that I should realise how lucky I am."

"He's funny."

"I asked him what he meant and he just smiled and walked away."

"Luisa, do you want dessert?" I ask, wanting to get her between the sheets.

"Be patient, Eric Morrison, we have only just finished our main. We aren't in a rush."

Try telling my cock that, I think, but of course don't say.

"Maybe we shouldn't have dessert, we are trying to save," I say weakly, I always sound weak when I try to lie to her.

"Eric, an extra £20.00 on top of what we have already spent isn't going to make a huge bit of difference, now is it? Now who's being all practical? Come, Eric, we need to both enjoy the moment. We have plans, yes, but sometimes I think you forget what is happening now. You have been drifting off in daydreams all day."

"I know. Let's enjoy tonight."

A waiter with a well-fitted suit comes over to clear our plates.

"Dessert menu?" he asks as his assistant pours us another glass of wine.

"Can you just give us a moment, please?" I ask as I squeeze Luisa's hand.

"Of course."

I'm not sure what we talk about for the rest of the meal. Pointless things mainly, but I guess sometimes being a little bit shallow can feel terribly refreshing.

"Come," I say as we finish our after-dinner drinks. "Let's go back to the room."

She giggles like a school girl as we help each other up the stairs.

The room is a deep pink with a round bed. "Champagne?" I say, opening the extortionately priced mini-bottle from the mini-bar.

"Eric, have we got the wrong room?" she says as the cork pops and I don't spill a drop.

"What?" I say, remembering that Luisa is wearing her black bra that I like. It undoes at the front.

"The bed is unmade."

"No, the staff have done that. It's all part of the service."

"That's funny."

"Oh, come here, Luisa. I love you so much," I say.

It's amazing what a bit of privacy can do for your sex life. This hotel is different; every corner of it is clean. The place makes us feel safe—like no one else can get into our world. We go through the Karma Sutra, our very own version. The sex is great. Better than with Rachel, better than the time that Betty Big Knockers first gave me head.

We sleep late the next morning and even manage to miss breakfast. I don't mind, we kind of need the rest. I am on cloud nine until Mickey and Mike pop like fat juicy zits straight into my mind, sticking to my thoughts and refusing to let me squeeze them away.

"Oh, don't be blue, baby," Luisa tells me, "we both don't have to be back at work until tonight." Luisa is soapy—she always forgets to rinse her back. I skim the towel over her soft skin.

"I know, but get dressed, honey, before they throw us out."

"We had a good time, though, didn't we, Eric."

"It was one of the best nights ever," I say, meaning every word of it.

We get back to the crap hotel and don't even make it into the hallway before Tim stops us.

"You two missed it big time here!" he says, smug with this fact. He doesn't wait for us to ask why, he just blabs out, "Fat Georg went mad! The police told him that his sister was murdered by her pimp and he just went crazy and smacked the copper straight in the mouth! He has been arrested."

"Oh!"we both say.

"Catch you later, Tim," I say as we run to our room, wanting to at least be allowed to ease back into it.

"See, Luisa, now can you understand why we had to get away from this place?"

She nods as we both get ready for work.

Pest

Today is full of hope. I am high as a kite and excitement lingers pleasantly, sticking to my every action. It has been weeks now and nothing from the journalist ... perhaps they just don't see me as good news anymore. I am pleased as I never said anything to Luisa. I am thankful, but try to resist the temptation to wonder how I would have been received by the newspaper-buying public. I guess I am not that famous anymore ... but the news has been dead for weeks, so surely I would have at least made it onto the back pages of some superficial chick magazine? The hundred grand would really help us, but that Mike guy must have changed his mind. Strange, though, as he seemed so keen that evening. He was real, wasn't he ... I'm not crazy, am I? I couldn't dream up something like that?

That doesn't matter, though, as today I am happy and it's the same feeling I can remember having as a child when I still believed in Santa. I had believed my mother when she told me that I had to go to sleep as he had just landed with my presents onto our roof and he wouldn't deliver them until I was fast asleep! Boy, did I try to sleep on those nights.

Rain clouds cause premature darkness to the sky. I am cold and as I walk quickly the tickets from the travel agent flap around in my pocket. They hold Luisa's and my future. Something so important in our plans is merely contained within a glossy envelope. Our journey printed onto two flimsy tickets. Twenty-four hours from today we will be heading to Spain by ferry. I am so lucky. I have a chance; I made that chance, though.

The flower seller stands outside the station looking pissed off. He obviously isn't following his dream. I feel a bit sorry for him as no one is stopping to buy a thing. No one is in the mood, I guess, since it's Monday evening and a work day. Everyone is skint. The smell I notice for the first time and remember it from when my mother was still alive. She always bought daffodils when it was spring. I grab a bunch of them and head off to meet Luisa from work. I will surprise her—she will expect me to be at home now, waiting for her. I just need to jump on the bus and I should be there in time to meet her. The bus roars out of nowhere, panting behind me. Why the hell don't people move out of the way if they see someone running? Lemmings, the lot of them.

"Move it, mate," I say as a woman in a tweed suit seems to just be walking in the middle of the path on purpose to slow me down! "Move it, thanks, it's too late! Thanks!" I shout as I miss my bus. She knows I am speaking to her, but is choosing to ignore me as she jumps in a taxi. If the next one isn't long I could still make it. London pisses me off sometimes. It's great for partying, but bad for your stress levels.

"Eric? Eric, waits for me, man?" Tim's voice shouts from behind

It's cold and I'm not in the mood to stand in the street and have small talk. If the next bus comes along I will still get it. I wish it would hurry up. Good old London transport is more than enough to turn the calm into the damn right crazy.

"Eric! Wait, man. I need to talk to you … it's important."

It's Tim. I was right; I had recognised his Hackney tone. He's running like a bull in a china stop, straight for me.

"Tim, how's it going?" I say falsely, wishing he would just leave me alone.

"It's OK, Eric. It's OK."

"Good, now what is it that is so important that you have chased me halfway down the street for?" The boy really could do with bathing more. He wonders why girls only go on one date before dumping him.

"I need to talk to you about something. It's about Luisa; there is something you should know."

"What's happened now?" I ask, thankful that this time tomorrow the drama of this place will be a memory; one that I will try with all my will to forget. "I'm in a hurry, Tim. What is it?" I say anxiously as my bus pulls up to the stop.

"Come, we can go into the Bull and I'll tell you over a drink."

"I have to get back and pack. Don't you remember, Luisa and I are moving to Spain tomorrow?" I ask and his face drops. The kid sees me as a brother, I guess. I feel a bit sorry for him as everyone always seems to take the piss out of him. I told him last night that it's only because they get a reaction out of him and he was to act like he didn't care, then they wouldn't bother him.

"No, shit, really? Spain, man … I would do anything to live there!"

I smile, as proud as the day when I first officially told everyone that I was a fully fledged record producer. The good times before Rachel sucked the life out of me. I'm not bitter, as Luisa has pumped it back into me.

"That's a shame, Eric—you and me were sound. I'm disappointed that I'm the last to know."

I'm not sure if he is joking as his statement is a little strange, but he laughs after a few seconds. His attempt at a little humour, I guess. I'm not sure why this is funny, but I grin back anyway. The boy looks fragile, breakable, like he has something inside that he wants to confide in me with and would if he didn't feel so soft for it. He can't get past the old me. I just want him for once to forget who I once was. I don't care now, so why should he?

"Eric, please, mate." He grabs my coat and I give him a nod to say yes.

"This round's on me!" he says, as if I have just given him a million pounds.

"I am only stopping for the one or Luisa will have my guts for garters," I say as my bus flies past and with it my chance to meet her. I guess we will be spending a lot of time together, so there is no need for me to meet her.

"Let me buy it, man," Tim insists as I reach for my wallet, "Look at it as a farewell present." He puts his arm around me and his stinks.

"Fine—Fine," I say, wondering what the hell I have in common with a kid whose main hero in life is Ali G. and who probably spends his Sunday mornings in bed waiting for *Hollyoaks* soap opera to start so he can have a wank over one of the girls' ample cleavage.

"I think what you did for Demetrius was amazing, Eric." Tim licks my backside as he buys me a beer and whiskey. I don't really drink whiskey, but I down it anyway. The place is smoky and full of mainly men. A grubby dog lies on the floor near our feet. If he was in a cartoon, the flies would be circling his head. It's not my local and I don't like the place. I want to be with Luisa and not here with some snotty-nose kid.

"If D's dad ever knew what happened," Tim continues,

"Well, let's not let him find out—for all our sakes! It's best you don't tell any of your friends what happened, just in case." He still won't make eye contact and bites at the corners of his filthy nails.

"I told my little brother, but he won't talk—he can't, he's deaf, you see." Tim wipes his nose on his sleeve. The snot lingers there and it makes me feel sick. The boy is a slob.

"Oh," I say, wanting him just to get to the point. "What is that you have to tell me about Luisa?" I say. "It's just I really need to be getting back."

"Oh, it's probably nothing."

I can't hide my, "Why the hell have you been wasting my time?" look and I can feel anger seeping out my eyes. My mother used to tell me that she could always tell when I was angry as I would glare at her like she was the devil. I don't like this.

"But I think you should know—all the same!" He adds, "What it is, you see, is that I think someone has been stalking her."

"Stalking her—what? She's never said anything to me."

"You know what she is like—she's a proud woman."

"Yes, but I would have thought she would say something about this to me." I feel hurt. "How come you think this?"

"The other day when I was covering the reception at the hotel for Cathy, whilst she was taking her break, something strange happened. Cathy's my girlfriend, in case you don't know. She's ginger, but still good-looking and her mother's got a bit of money. Buys her expensive clothes. Yeah, Cathy's all right even if she has a ginger muff."

"I've not met her," I say.

"We have just started going out. I was covering for her when I see from the window that Luisa is coming down the street. She is walking quickly and keeps looking behind her. A tall man dressed in a black coat and with a hooded top pulled up by his eyes appears to be following her. And before you say, it's not just one of those coincidences … it can't be, for every time she looks around, the man dives into shop doorways or pretends to look in a window. When she does eventually make it through the door, the man stops outside and writes down the phone number from the hotel sign and then goes."

"When did this happen?" I say, annoyed at Luisa and him for keeping this from me.

"Last Tuesday."

"Why didn't you call me?"

"I didn't have any proof and you would have just panicked and called the pigs. The pigs don't give a shit—there is nothing that they can do."

"At least if I had known I wouldn't have left her alone … like I have now! I have to go; she is walking home on her own and it's got dark early!"

"Wait, Eric, there is more."

"What."

"For the last week, I's been following her. Watching that she has been OK. Every night that man has been behind her. I even tried to catch him once. You know, to give him what for. But he's big, Eric; he has muscles the size of truck tires."

"Tim, are you definitely sure about this?"

"Man, why would I be putting you through this if I wasn't sure. That's why I've waited until now to say anything! You know how I can be a little paranoid, but when he started to camping out in a black Volvo opposite every night—I knew I was right. One day the phone kept going in the hotel. Every time Luisa picked it up there was no one at the other end. It happened three or four times before I could convince her to let me answer it. Your Luisa can be very proud, you know. But still, she can handle herself. Anyway, I shouted at this man down the phone telling him that I knew exactly what he had been up to and that if he didn't leave Luisa alone, I would call the police. Your misses thought I was a little crazy, I think. I don't mind, it's not as if I couldn't turn around to her and say, well, I's a been following you for days and this guy is stalking you!"

"Shit, I really need to go." Tim ignores me.

"Still, you are moving to Spain tomorrow, you say, and away from weirdos like that."

"Tim, I don't know what to say."

"Don't worry—I know you are busy. I just thought you should know."

"I need to get back to her."

"Shit—yes, you must. I shouldn't have kept you this long. But if you could wait just one minute whilst I take a piss, I will walk back with you. I'm taking the bird to see the new George Clooney film tonight and I'm already ten minutes late for her."

I sit there panicking as the boy goes to pee. Tim's a little strange, but hey, he's a good boy at heart. I feel bad for being so rude with him earlier.

"Ready?" he says, returning before I have had time to take it in.

"Yes," I reply and we grab our coats and head out into the sharp spring air.

"Want a fag?" he asks, lighting me one before I have had the chance to answer.

"Thanks!" I say. The wind is blowing and fine rain is falling. The tickets feel like a weight in my pocket. If my coat doesn't hold off the rain they could be ruined. I pick up the pace.

Tim, on the other hand, slows right down and keeps turning over his shoulder. He is taking himself a little too serious, I think. I can't see anyone.

"Tim, step on it, will you—I don't want to get my tickets wet."

"I am really, really sorry, mate."

"What?" I say.

"It's him, Eric. Look over the road—he's the one who has been stalking your Luisa!"

"Really?" I say as a man whose face I can't make out stares at us from the other side of the road. He wasn't there a minute ago ... I don't see how I could have missed him.

"That's the guy," Tim continues proudly and before any logic has time to spring to mind—I am running over the road to catch him. Tim starts to run, but in a different direction—probably got some plan to catch the man from around a different road. But then the man changes direction and begins to run in the same direction as Tim. Tim hasn't noticed. Shit, what if he is trying to kill him for letting me know!

I can see him and Tim are not far ahead. I guess when the right moment presents itself Tim will notice he is being followed. Tim must be thinking he can head the guy up at the end of one of the streets. I wish he would notice that he is being followed ... for his sake.

This should all be over soon and the man will wish he never messed with me. Tim should turn around soon and give the man what for ...

I gasp for breath as we continue with our chase for what must be twenty minutes. Despite the sharp night, sweat is dripping off my chin and my ears are burning in the way they always did as a kid when forced to perform PE and other winter sports, battering against cold northern winds. The rows of Victorian houses end as we head into a mountain of a housing estate. Each row of blocks becomes more and more disorientating until I'm running down an alleyway. Its lights are sparser then anywhere else. I hear arguments and then the sound of an almighty thud.

"Tim, are you all right, mate? Tim?" I turn on my heels, searching for my mobile, my hands shaking as I begin to dial the police.

"Eric, help me!" a weak-voiced Tim tries to shout. "Eric, help me."

"I'm just calling the old bill," I shout down the corridor.

"No—wait—I have already done it. I just need you to come and help me—help me—my ankle is broken."

"Tim, I can't see you, mate," I shout. "Where is the man? Did you get him?"

"Just walk in a straight line—you can't miss me. You will see when you get here. Just hurry up—I need you, Eric—more than you know."

"I'm coming, mate!" Using my hands to feel my way, I walk to save Tim. The man is a hero as far as I am concerned.

"Tim," I say, "did you get him, Tim?" I can hear deep breathing and the whisk of piss licks across my nostrils.

"Yes, you are close now. Just keep coming this way."

"Tim, I want to thank you for all your help. Luisa will be so grateful. You know, if I am going to be honest, she thinks you are a bit flaky, but after today she will give you the respect you deserve."

BANG... a hit ... damn ... my head ... off. ...

Unfairness

It's the early hours before I come to. I know that because my watch lights up on the hour. I have an egg erupting out of the back of my head. Some bastard knocked me out. I am worried, for there is no sign of Tim or the other guy. Perhaps Tim is in trouble. I would call the police, but my phone has gone along with my wallet, my cigarettes, and even my coat! I can hear kids laughing. This place is a shit hole. I smell like piss. I must have landed in it. This must be a dirty bastard's piss alley. Dirty, smelly, animal humans whipping out their stinking dicks just because they are too lazy to wait until they get home.

My ankle fucking kills. The last time it felt like this was when I fell funny at football. I reckon I might have sprained it. Just my luck. Luisa will have to drive tomorrow. She won't like that. She's a shit driver. We will be lucky to get there in one piece. We always argue when she's behind the wheel. I can't relax when someone else is driving. When I was seventeen my best friend's girlfriend was killed in a car crash. My mate was driving her home. I was too pissed to drive. He was pissed as well, but since he did it every week, none of us noticed anymore. A cat ran into the road and Rebecca had said something like "mind the cat." He had swerved the steering wheel, but in doing so had turned too quickly and Rebecca wasn't belted in like we were and she flew through the window until a wooden fence broke her fall by impaling itself through her heart.

Her parents wouldn't let us go to the funeral. I wasn't driving the car that killed her, but they wouldn't let any of her friends go to say goodbye. Since then I haven't been in a car with a driver that I didn't trust. I don't miss Rebecca, I didn't really like her and my friend was about to dump her before she died. I still think it was unfair, though; but she should have belted up.

Dragging myself to my feet, waves of conversation bounce off the walls until I pin their source and hobble toward it. It keeps moving, like it's trying to tease me and take the piss out of my leg. Still, I can't keep it up; it can't fool me as I am headed the right way.

"Oy! You lot," I shout as boys' voices battle against each other, despite the hour. "Where the fuck is my stuff?" Of course they don't look at me. There must be about ten of them. They could easily beat me up if they all tried. Only their coats are visible to me. The darkness shades their faces except for their teeth, which glow like tusks in the crappy street light.

"I'm talking to you lot! Who the fuck stole my stuff??" They stare at me. I might be about to die. I don't feel that bothered. I don't think this is really going to happen. I might get a punch at the worst. Still, there are so many more of them than there is of me, so maybe I will be dancing with the grim reaper later.

"Fuck off, wanker!" they say. "Fuck off!" They all turn their backs and go. Maybe they are fed up of waiting around in the rain, or is it more to do with the fact that someone has called the police as sirens sing in the distance. I would hate to be so poor that I lived in a place like this. The hotel is a dive as well, but this place is a bigger, more concentrated, cemented collection of misery. The boys have run off. I think there is one girl with them as she has long hair and a short skirt. She's trailing behind. They leave her and I guess she must go home. Not once do any of them look back at me. I don't seem to move until I can no longer hear their voices. I should have held my temper. Now I am stuffed. The place is silent as if I am the last man in the universe. The police car mustn't be headed my way. I think I could live with this, just me and Luisa as the new Adam and Eve of this world. People say I am pessimistic since I lost my career; maybe I am, but life isn't exactly a good advert or a promoter of happiness. If something good happens, you can bet your life that something bad will be around the corner.

It's late and I have to get back to Luisa. When I get back I will check with Demetrius that Tim is OK. There is no need to involve the old bill for that will just bring us all trouble, and Tim should be all right and I haven't got time to answer their questions. Nothing is going to delay me getting away. Luisa and I are going to escape the disease of this place before we get permanently infected.

My foot kills. Each step is more painful. Jesus, this is a shit night. I am going to have to get cab. I can't walk it. Luisa can pay the cab at the other end.

An old-fashioned phone box, red like a beacon, is presented like a peace offering from the gods, just over the road, next to the nicer houses. A cat spits at me as I disturb its path. I would kick the thing, but if karma is true then that might be my granny inside there and I could come back as a slug.

The interior of the booth is warm, but the phone has no handle. I could cry. I really could.

How the hell am I going to explain this to Luisa? I best just check on her then call into Demetrius to check Tim. If she is pissed I will get Tim to explain why I have been out for half the night. I sit on a wall; the only hope is for the police to spot me. My head hurts a lot.

Then God sends me an angel in the shape of Rosie Walls. Rosie is cab driver who sometimes comes into my local, not that I have drank in there much since dating Luisa.

"All right, Eric?" she asks as I flag her down. Rosie looks like her name. She dresses in jeans and T-shirt, but her headscarf and elaborate gold jewelry makes her look just like a fortune teller.

"I've been mugged, Rosie, and I can't afford to pay you until I get home."

"Are you OK?" she asks.

"No, not really, my ankle is painful and I have had a terrible night."

"Eric, this one's on me. I was going home anyway and I pass by your place. Look at it as a leaving present."

"Shit, the tickets! They have stolen my tickets for tomorrow," I say, not even saying thank you.

"Call the police when you get in. They won't be able to use them."

"Thanks, Rosie, you came along at the right time."

"Yes, I don't normally travel home this way, but something made me try a different way. Well, if I am to be honest, I couldn't remember if it was Sycamore Street or Sinclair Street down this way and I wanted to refresh my memory." She giggles as I stagger into the back.

"Take care, Rosie," I say, planting a kiss on her forehead in lieu of payment. I will invite her to stay in Spain once we are settled.

"Bye-bye."

The room is in darkness as I go in. Only the faint light from the moon is there to guide me to my princess; guide me to our last night on this bed. Of course, she is sleeping, probably gave up waiting up half the night. I don't want to disturb her before I know Tim is all right. Just one cuddle before I wake Demetrius; just one kiss before I plough further into the night. I slide next to her. She is cold and slimy. Shit, she is wet! The bed is damp and cold. I don't know how I can clean her up without waking her. I can't leave her in it. Shit, what's wrong with her? I will just have to come clean after all. I haven't done anything wrong and she will understand why I have been so long.

She's never done anything like this; it's probably caused by just nerves, for I know that she doesn't like traveling. I know that much. She's pissed off with me. I don't blame her.

I shake at her, but she is cold. Colder than cold—as cold as a dead, frozen fish.

"Luisa!" I scream, but in my heart I already know that it is much too late. Her flesh is numb. I stretch to reach it, but the bedside light isn't there. So I go to the wall way over on the other side of the room. There is a breeze and the curtain flaps like a sail. It's not like Luisa to sleep in this weather, with the window open. There is something terribly wrong about this whole thing.

My foot cuts on broken glass? Something sharp? Limping on both legs now, I switch slides on and the room lights up like an atrium. Like an entry for the Turner art prize. But it is not the sight of my beautiful girlfriend that turns my insides into frozen milk; no, it's the fact that her naked body is lying on a platter of blood and our once-white sheets. The cotton is encircling her like raspberry swirls on top of a Starbucks coffee of the month, each layer getting more intense colours of red as it reaches the middle. Her soft skin has been sliced with deep knife marks or some sort of sharp thing, sharp enough to rip into her delicate, beautiful insides. She is dead, all right—as dead as she will ever be. Dead as the previous day. Her eyes gaze at me as if to tell me what I already know—someone has been here and gone long before I got home. I look at my hands and her metallic-scented blood stains my fingers like blackberry juice spilt onto wool. We are the only people on this floor at the moment as Georg has been doing it up. If she screamed then no one would have heard her.

This can't be happening to me; my world has now stopped and I wish to God that my heart would do the same.

I am living a nightmare.

I should call 999. Get the police to come, get an ambulance maybe to try and re-start her heart, but she has been dead for a while.

"Luisa!

"Police, Please.
I Want to Report a Murder."

I'm not sure when they all arrived. I don't even know who sorted out the phone call. Maybe it was D. It doesn't matter, as the police are everywhere. Like a swarm of bees they take over the place, propping up every doorway as their radios crack words that I don't want to hear. My bedroom is fenced with luminous banners, marking off the scene. Luisa's blood stains my hands and I know what they are thinking … Morrison has done it again.

"Come on, Mr. Morrison," one of them says to me. I haven't been listening so far.

"You have to come with us now."

"Sure," I say wanting them to hit me, to beat me into pulped tomatoes. I should have gotten that bus. They could have at the very least sprayed pepper spray into my face, stung my eyes out like they do in the movies. I want one of them to shoot me (if only they carried guns). He could say it was in self-defense or something. No one would care. Some might even say that it would be a way of saving the tax payer's money. One less wanker to house in a prison. *Shoot me now!* my insides scream, *blow my brains out like meat balls.*

To my disappointment, the police are surprisingly civilised to me and I have no choice, then, but to let Luisa slide from my grip like a sacrificial bride being given to the wolves to devour. Only she's already dead and it is my fault.

They put a blanket over my head. The TV cameras are outside. I hate the press and they hate me. The car journey is fast and again I am being led into the police station undercover.

I won't talk when they get me in there. I am seeing, breathing, hearing and have all the signs of being alive, but this isn't living. I find that every time I try to speak to the officer my diaphragm contracts and I'm short of breath. The only words I manage to say are, "I didn't do it." They think I am a fruit cake—made up of nuts and with thoughts contrived of sweetly sick syrup.

I am not sure what happens after this, as it's all a bit of a mystery, as I wake up in a police cell and I am wearing blue trousers and I can't remember changing my clothes. Somehow we have reached mid-morning and I have lost time. I could tear my sheet into strips and hang myself by the neck. They check me now and again, but if I wait until later then I could do it. I did do it to her in a way, you know, I mean, I should have been there. I guess if I kill myself they will think I have done it. I don't believe in killing yourself, so they have nothing to worry about. If they don't get the man he could do it again and Luisa would be cross with me. Luisa, I wish you would wake me up and tell me that this is nothing but a bad, bad dream.

She won't come though, for I deserve my nightmare.

When they do eventually interview me it's late afternoon at about the time when Luisa and I should have been on our way to Spain. We had lived all year for this day. With each extra shift we crammed into our already chocked week we told ourselves that it would be worth it as soon we would be free. We were to ride into the orangey Seville sun and procreate under the scent of olive groves; living happily ever after in a perfect world. But now this is dead.

As I sit down opposite the two officers, the room starts to consume me. The horrible artificial light shows up everything and the man opposite me is suffering with a bad case of adult acne. He is stocky and with salt and pepper hair. His voice is as gruff as a dog bark. I try to stop looking at his skin, for I have a spot myself. I resist the urge to squeeze as all eyes are on me. My chest feels a thud as the other ginger coloured officer with the bad teeth presses the grey record button. I have to admit that it doesn't look good for me now, does it? Two murdered girlfriends under suspicious circumstances. If I was a jury I would be pointing the finger firmly at me. If Luisa hadn't met me, then surely she would still be alive. I am at the point now where there isn't anything else that you could throw at me. You can't break someone who already feels broken, now can you?

The press will have a field day. My face is probably splashed over every paper in the country.

The stories will be something like:

"Shamed record producer, Eric Morrison, was arrested in the early hours of this morning after police were called to a disturbance at his North London hotel room. Mr. Morrison was found clutching the dead body of his girlfriend, Luisa Cicona. Miss Cicona was a twenty-eight-year-old waitress and had been his girlfriend for the last few years.

Eric is now being held at Islington Police Station. Edward Woods, the officer in charge of the investigation, has no comment to make at present.

Back in 1999, Eric was also arrested in connection with the brutal murder of the star Rachel Garbo, after she was found dead at their London home. He was never charged as there was insufficient evidence and apparently a fourth unknown DNA sample was found. Some are calling for the case to be re-opened. See page seven for a full account of the rise and fall of this once household name."

"Mr. Morrison, are you listening?" the officer shouts.

"Yes, yes."

"Well, can we start?"

My mouth moves, but I'm not really listening to what I am telling them. I don't want to hear.

As I tell my tale, they seem to want more, every last detail of what happened that night. The interviewer raises his voice, asks me again and again if I killed her. My solicitor butts in and tells him that I have no comment or something to that word. It's a game with this law and order business and it's one that I have lost interest in. They are wasting their time with me when they could be out finding out who really killed her. I want to tell them this, but my better sense keeps me quiet.

Back at the cell I'm given a meal. It's battery breed chicken that tastes as if it has just come out of a microwave. Chicken chucked into a thick brown sauce. I eat, though, for I am famished. My stomach gurgles like a baby. There is also some sort of pink blancmange on my tray. It looks like it's been dropped or maybe even passed through someone's stomach. I haven't eaten food like this since I was at school. It tastes OK, but I know they have dropped it. Even the orange juice looks like piss.

Time elapses unhurriedly, like a relentless winter, and I have little to do with my day other then play football with a rogue pea that's made it onto the floor. It's a good game for all of about five minutes, then I manage to squash it. It looks like a green bogey. A splattered martian, a squashed frog.

I wish I could escape. End it now, press the eject button on life, but that would make me a coward. For, like I said, I have never understood and have up until now never been able to relate to why people kill themselves. The cops had no worries about that last night. Jesus, the pain they must feel, for I think all death must hurt … poor Luisa—did death hurt a lot? Then there is the poor sod that has to find you. Surely the sight of a corpse would stay with them for the rest of their life? I've heard that the carbon dioxide in the car method leaves you with your eyes popped out like corks. Imagine opening up your garage to find that greeting you? Imagine if it's a kid that finds you or some old lady? They could die of fright. Yes, generally I feel suicide is selfish, but I do understand why people end up with nowhere else to go but down this road.

What am I going to do now? I don't want another woman. What can I do for the rest of my time?

Luisa, please haunt me, please stay with me and keep me with hope.

A pig with a handful of keys opens up my cell door. I almost smile when I am told that I have been given bail. My solicitor has sorted it out with my cousin. He then drives me to a hotel, all the time telling me that I should "take it easy."

It's a discreet place as he thinks it's best I hide since half the press are camped out like hounds—wanting to eat me.

The place is OK; in fact, it's a bit posh for me nowadays. But I don't like the way it has been designed ... the whole place pretends to be your friend just for the night, with its mini-bar and welcome pack and lists of movies to view. However, its one mission is to get your money and then it is so quick to forget you the next morning after it's been primed and gleamed ready for the next guest. Well, it's not going to fool me, not once. It can go to hell.

Two weeks later the room is seriously pissed off that it has had to be nice to me for all this time. The movies don't change much. The restaurant food is too rich for me, so I just eat their sandwiches.

I haven't slept since it happened. It is awful and apparently the guests complain that I scream all through the night. So they send for a doctor, paid for by the tax payer who just wants to string me up. It takes the old boy all of ten minutes to decide that I am having some stress-related breakdown.

"We just need to take you away from it all for a bit ... it should help," the doc tells me.

"But I thought that was why they brought me here?"

"Trust me, OK. Things will work out."

So I am made to stay in a nut house in case I try to top myself! As if.

Luisa, you kissed me last night, didn't you? You kissed my lips and then floated away.

I wait for you, have done so for ages. I even leave my bedside light on in case you have lost your way. A month I wait for you to return, but you haven't been back since they gave me those wonderful drugs. They don't make me forget you, but I do go through my days wondering if this is what life has left for me ... escapism and the protection of plenty of nurses to tend to my every need. Maybe I could try to fake madness, spend the rest of my days swaying in a chair and making someone spoonfeed my dinner. But despite movies like *One Flew Over The Cuckoo's Nest* and books like *Veronica Decides to Die,* these doctors actually know their stuff and can't be fooled, not for one bit. It's a shame, for I feel safe here, but I know that soon I will have to go.

The drugs are wonderful, you know. They really help to ease the pain. The gardens are peaceful, you know, but are full of the crazy and insane. I even like the game room, playing Connect Four with some of the maddest residents, whom in a blink of an eye can throw the game against the wall. Other days they can play with me for hours, even if I do beat them. Some of the nurses are nice, usually the male ones. The woman nurses look at me like the rest of the public, but half the time I just ignore it.

"We are sending you home, Mr. Morrison," Dr. Wilburn tells me at my assessment. Six months or so into my sentence. It's not right ...

"But I don't have a home to go to," I say honestly. "There is nothing left for me."

"Tough," I am told, "this is not a holiday camp." And I am shown the way out.

I move into a flat this time as I can't stay in another hotel. The flat is given to me by the council. Thanks, guys, but could you have picked a shittier place? Its walls are rice paper thickness and it gives less privacy then my last hotel room. Good job I don't fuck anymore. Good job all I do is watch TV all day.

I'm down again as they have reduced my drugs. I try to be positive and thankful for being alive, but some wanker raped my Luisa and stole our future. Some wanker forced his ugly, unloved willy in between her beautiful fur and spat right into our unborn baby's face. Yes, they found out in the autopsy that she was carrying our child. They didn't tell me at first as they didn't think I could take it. They are right, but the anger is undesirable and I wonder if there is a chance I could dedicate my life to hunting down her killer. When I find out who did it, could I rip their heart from the chest as they have done so to mine?

Ring, ring.

My phone goes, but I am reluctant to answer it for it only ever brings me bad news.

"Eric?"

It's my solicitor.

"Yes?"

"Eric, can I come over—I have news for you."

"So, what is new, then? Am I to go to trial soon now that I am better?"

"I have to talk to you."

"Blimy—this must be super-duper news!" I say sarcastically, as this always makes him so flustered.

"It is. I will be around in twenty minutes," he says.

I should really clear up the place, move the beer cans that have accumulated since lunchtime and hide the fact that I am into snorting lines of coke. The guy next door gets it. He's a full-time drug dealer, but loves his kids. Tells me if he ever catches anyone giving them any of the shit that we take that he would bury them alive!

I can't be bothered to clean, though, for what is Derek going to say? I don't care. I should clean my teeth. I can't stand morning breath, even if it is three in the afternoon.

A sharp knock makes my nerves leap. It's only ten minutes since we spoke—I bet he was parked outside all the time!

"Come in, Derek, the door is open," I shout from the bathroom through mouthfuls of toothpaste.

"Jesus, Eric, this place is a state. Do you want me to get someone to come and clean it up?" This guy has an obsession with cleanliness.

"No thanks—you're already eating into the money my cousin was supposed to hold for me and not give to me no matter how hard I begged him. If I start sticking extra cleaning charges onto my bill, I will be lucky to be able to afford a packet of crisps when I'm old." My words are sharp, but I hate the fact he pretends to be on my side. He just wants my money.

"What, do you expect me to work for you for nothing?" he says. Scratching at his nose.

"Derek—I'm just in a cynical mood—ignore me. I am at a bad place."

"Well, sitting around drinking beer all day isn't going to help."

"I know—that's one of the first things Luisa said to me."

"She sounded like she was a bright lady."

"She was so bright, Derek, that her body glowed in the dark. But you aren't here to talk about what an amazing girl Luisa was, are you? So lets cut the shit, shall we—what is it that is so important that you had to drive over to tell me?"

"They have found the killer."

"What? Who is it—give me the name of the sick fucker and I will tear him limb from limb."

"It was Tim Hercules."

"Tim! Tim killed her! But he's missing. Did they ever find him after that night? He's the one who warned me about a stalker—you remember what I told you at the office of how he had pointed out a tall man with a skin head in red puffer jacket?"

"Yes, but it turns out the stalker was from CID. He was also murdered that night and was found yesterday in the attic of Tim's grandmother. The poor lady had been living at her sister's, who was sick for the last six months; she only came home after she died. Didn't have a clue—said she could smell something awful and had complained for two weeks, but no one would listen until her son went up to investigate. The CID man had been following Tim, as he suspected him of being a heavy drug dealer. Tim murdered him."

"I don't know what to say!" I say. "He's a bastard, a deceitful, evil little bastard."

I cry after this. Cry, cry and cry.

"Don't bother with the tea, I can see you need some time to take it in. Give me a call in the morning," Derek says, running for the hills.

"I want to see him—I want to rip his fucking throat off," I demand.

"That's going to be a little difficult on the count that he's been dead for two months."

"And when were you going to tell me this, Derek?" He looks uncomfortable and too bloody rightfully so. I hate solicitors, they are like estate agents … leeches of the world.

"Killed himself the day after he killed Luisa," he continues. "They found him yesterday buried under his granddad's compost heap at the allotment; apparently he crawled in with the muck, then took an overdose."

"Fitting death for an evil wanker."

"I don't want to tell you this, but I guess you are going to find out anyway. … He was wearing a personal stereo and the tape inside was you. The Orange Mens' last album. He also had posters all over his wall at home."

"Fucking prick." I kick the table in temper.

"Look, Eric, you are going to have to calm down. Calm down. You are off the hook—and he's dead. You need time alone to take it all in, but for God's sake, calm down. Now, are you going to be all right on your own, or should I get one of the guys to look in later."

"Just go, Derek. Just go," I say.

I don't sit in my flat, instead, I pull on a hood top and go for a walk. No one will be expecting me to do so and besides, with the hood up, I look like anyone else.

I walk along the edge of Tower Bridge. The place has a smog of tourists, despite the coldness. They don't know me and I blend like cream into the picture as I walk and smoke. The only option I have now is to wreak my revenge in the afterlife. I am willing to go to hell for Luisa if it means I can hunt him down. But like I said, I can't kill myself—instead, I will have to wait for my life to trickle away—but one day I will get him.

An elderly couple smile at me as I squeeze to let them past. If only the rest of the world could view me as simply a human being and not this distorted monster who likes to murder his girlfriends for entertainment. How could I have been so stupid in the first place to believe the shit that Tim fed me? Only a fool would have been taken in by him. A couple go by and a girl with the same silly blonde hair and light olive skin as Luisa laughs as her boyfriend scoops her in his arms. She could be Luisa's sister and I want with all my heart to touch her, to have her for the night. They pass quickly and her perfume tickles me as I walk on for the rest of the night. Even her scent is the same.

The police report shows that Tim had an obsession with me. His walls at home, like Derek said, were covered from head to toe in pictures of me or anything related to me. Apparently, once whilst appearing on Top of the Pops I had given him a look down the TV— a look that for some reason had made him think he was special. I am not sure how they know this—well, it had said as much in his diary. He didn't look like the sort of boy to keep such a thing. I could see him being the sort that could barely read. He came across as stupid, but at school they tell me he had always got straight A's in chemistry.

In his bedroom they found the most unsettling picture—one taken a few weeks before it all happened—one of Luisa and me asleep in our room. They think he snuck into our room one night. Apparently he believed he owned me, and killed Luisa, for he thought she was stealing me away. Sick fucker—I can't begin to understand—I am told it is best not to, but I know one thing, if he hadn't have killed himself, I would have done it for him, all right! Glad he climbed under the shit to die.

Clean Living

Six months later and I still haven't managed to escape from the filth. It climbs the damp walls of my apartment, it pollutes my ears, and it collects like phlegm at the back of my throat. If I scrub my body, even with a wooden brush, it still scents my skin. It's shitting on everything and there is nothing, it seems, that I can do to stop it.

Maybe I am all cleared now in the world of *The Sun* and *Daily Mail* reader. I'm almost liked since they found out it was Tim and not me. I even had a few offers of work. I've been told that the publicity has made it good for me to have a comeback. I haven't bought a CD in ages; how the fuck would I know what is in and what is out? The radio is OK, but I don't really listen to much of that nowadays. In the paper yesterday they were trying to insinuate that Tim could have killed Rachel. The obsession thing has really got the public going. I don't want to spoil it for them, but we all know that this isn't the case. I didn't even know Tim then. People are funny creatures; they seem to always be obsessed with conspiracies and murders. Most people love a good murder case—they love the fact that they have something to fill their TV soap-filled lives with for a few weeks. It gives them something to talk about other than just *East Enders* or *Jerry Springer*. God, I watch that now.

We aren't progressing, you know! Don't let them tell you that we are, because we aren't! We were up until about 1970, since then we have been stepping backward. Soon the whole world will be filled with nothing but hundreds of fat kids. Soon their stench and the stench of others will not be able to be cleaned from our noses. Computer games and Big Macs, that's all the future has to offer. It's a good job I won't ever breed. Why would I want to after learning all this?

I am also regressing. I'm not blameless in all this. Most things in my life have gone back to how they were before Luisa and I got it together. I don't work. Cero said I could work in his kitchen, for no one would see me back there; but I can't do that for the rest of my life, or for even a day. I have areas and I don't mix much with people, other than the odd stranger, and I don't even have a local. I am sure there is one, but since I have moved to South London, I don't have any friends at all. I'm watching crap TV. I am also sort of kidding myself, finding it easier to believe that, after all, I'm nothing more than a pig at heart and extremely lost without a woman to organise me—I know men of my generation aren't supposed to admit this—but it's the truth. Well, it's easier if this is the truth, anyhow. I don't just want any woman, I don't want a substitute. I just want Luisa; she is all that I need. She has been taken from me and I can't just forget.

Still, bad as it is, I have slept with others since Luisa—I don't believe she would want it any other way. Maybe I would not understand if it was the other way around. I admit I have double standards—but the silly truth is that I am one of those people who just can't live without sex. I think it is a normal function and one that everyone takes far too seriously. The girls I have been shagging are the same sort as me. I picked them up at a bar, a different one every time. It's easier this way. I wouldn't want the responsibility of the same thing happening again—after all, the world is safer without me having a girlfriend. I don't kiss them; I don't even see them as women. I just use them and abuse them. I never take them back to mine. I always go to theirs so I can run out of the room when they are in the bathroom cleaning up. I'm a wanker. They are not Luisa and never can be.

I just need to discover where to go next. I'm hoping (for you have to have hope, if nothing else) that this slob business is just a metamorphosis period for me and that maybe I will soon change into something brand new. The problem is that I don't have much incentive (again) as I have dole coming in, which is enough to pay for my simple ways. I don't buy anything.

I'm a bit worried as this screaming thing has come back. Last week, the pain it left in my chest seemed to have lasted for days. I'm back on the tablets, but they don't work as well as they used to. Luisa's pain-filled body visits me every night. I know she isn't real, but it doesn't stop me from seeing her. She has started to decay now, her skin is rotted and half-peeled away. Yesterday she lost a finger when she was talking to me and even slung a few maggots onto my bed as she bent down to read the paper. I tried to pretend it didn't happen, as I know she would be embarrassed by this, but I don't want to ask her to leave. It wouldn't be fair. She asked me to kiss her before she went, but I didn't want to do it. I had to be honest and told her that if I did that her jaw may fall off or even her teeth. She didn't speak to me after I said this to her. Can you see why I let the maggot thing go? I can see why she might feel just a bit insecure. In the end, she settled for a peck on her hand. It felt like papier-mâché and great chunks flaked onto my lips. She began to cry as I ran into the bathroom to rinse my mouth. God knows what a state she will be in next time she wants to come and see me. Still, I want to see her, but I think soon she won't be able to work here. I know she isn't real, but I still like to see her.

Padding Out

I don't really do religion. I'm just not convinced. I want to do it—get it like Luisa did with her Catholic stuff, but I just can't make myself believe it. Mum and Dad used to take me to church at Christmas and Easter when I was a kid. I remember the giant stone walls and the cold breeze that would whistle under the door in winter. I was always too small to see well, so we had to sit right at the front. The vicar would stare at me and I would always forget the words of the hymns. I felt he could tell that I was not really feeling this and simply an imposter, a horrible little boy with a heart too rigid and with bad parents who thought that going at Easter and Christmas made up for all their absence the rest of the year.

I had a friend once who had no doubt in his mind that he was one hundred percent a Christian; he even managed to drag me along to one of his wacky, trendy church services. Everyone was nice, the girls weren't bad either, but still I didn't feel anything. It still didn't feel real. Occasionally I have felt like maybe there could be a God there, for who is doing all this stuff and how the hell did we get here if this isn't the case? But that's only occasionally and the way I see God isn't as this little old man dressed in old-fashioned white robes with blue eyes and white skin. I see God as a sexless being, more a life force, a happening, just like the wind and the sun and the earth. Even this I'm not sure about. I hope Luisa is in a place known as heaven, for it must be a really big place to fit in so many people. Maybe it grows with the people. I can kind of see the Buddhist belief that we are re-born, for that would be a far more economical way to deal with life and it would mean there would be a lot more space in heaven. Luisa might be growing in someone's stomach right now, waiting to come into the world. Only I can't see this, since she is haunting me. My understanding is that when someone haunts you it's because they have some sort of unfinished business to deal with. I think Luisa is pissed off with me. Or perhaps I am a little crazy.

Anyway since I can't do the religion thing and find myself and I can't kill myself, what am I going to do all day? I could turn to drugs, but I already take them. I want to take too much or let them take over my life, but I can't. Dope makes my throat hurt if I smoke it too much and unless I become a thief (which isn't in my nature), I can't afford more than the odd line of cocaine. I may start knitting, but that would make me a bit of a drip, and I can't paint, or build, or fix, or make anything other then music. I can't afford the music equipment and no one will give me another chance since I went in the nut house (if, of course, I wanted a chance). I don't want to work back at the restaurant as Luisa haunts that place as well and if I was there she would haunt me all day long and I would drive everyone crazy with my crazy way of shouting and stuff. Yes, the rest of my days will now be dedicated to watching TV at the tax payers' expense. The way I see it, I must have paid the average tax payers' tax three, maybe four times over, so it's now time for me to claim it back.

I am going to get fat. Bloat my stomach out like a water balloon. I want to fill the room with blubber. If I start off with a box of donuts and then increase it by two boxes, it shouldn't take more than about ten years before the slime sticks to my arteries. I plan to fill this room with my blubber. Blubber boy, *Oi, fatty!* they will say to me and no one will have a clue who I am. Women won't touch me, which means it will be easier for me to stay faithful to Luisa.

The next morning I go around to the local bakery. It's not Queenie's Oven, but the owners aren't too un-similar. This one's called Betty and has nicotine-stained teeth. Her blouse wraps her fifty-year-old bosoms. Everyone she speaks to she addresses as "pet." She's a Geordie and time hasn't softened her accent.

"What can I get you, pet?" she asks.

"A box of your donuts," I ask brightly.

"A whole box? I hope they aren't all for you," she kids.

"No, for the boys in the van. You better make it two boxes, as you know how we builders like to eat."

"I do, indeed! We open for bacon butties at seven if you are passing. I do wicked bacon and egg doorstep."

"Sounds good. Sounds good."

"Right there, pet," she says, giving me an extra donut in one of the boxes.

"Come back again," she tells me.

"Oh, I will, I will."

I get home and open my donuts. A detective series is on the Hallmark Channel. The plot is obvious; it is the wife who is the killer of her husband. She found out he was having an affair and in a fit of rage she battered him to death. She doesn't want to lose her large house with the heated swimming pool and tennis and squash courts. Her sister-in-law is suspicious, so the woman also kills her. The rookie detective, however, isn't buying any of it and after a series of life-threatening situations, he manages to expose the woman. However, she has too much pride to go to jail and jumps from her balcony straight to her death. That's the right thing to watch, I guess, if I want to watch something un-taxing. The first three donuts go down a treat. I am hungry, so eating them isn't too much bother. They slide down my gullet like gentle rounds of butter. The fourth is a little difficult and the fifth just isn't going down there. I have to admit that I am extremely disappointed! I mean, it isn't hard, is it? I should be able to eat four. I have another eight to try and eat. If I stop eating when I am full I am never going to become a couch potato. I force the next seven down. I force and force and force despite the gags and the pain in my belly. I sit there and I'm proud I have eaten so many. The last donut sits there. I'll eat him just before I go to bed. I want him to lie on my stomach and eat away at my heart. It's not really killing yourself, now is it? You wouldn't dare accuse a smoker of committing a slow, drawn-out suicide, now would you? You wouldn't dare tell a fat person that they were purposely taking their own life, now would you? You would get sued for daring to even think it. Alcoholics and drug addicts are the same. Mind you, they do get a hard time. A Valium addict, on the other hand, will find it easier to keep their addition secret.

Yes, I had an addiction once in the name of Rachel Garbo. If I can harness that feeling again, then maybe I would have a chance. Each time I see a donut I will pretend it is Rachel. Each time I pass a McDonald's or Burger King I will pretend there are millions of her sizzling away. Smoking and flame grilling. Rachel cheese, Rachel bread roll, Rachel ketchup.

Of course, this is a bit weird … I do realise that. But somehow it works and less than a month later I am a whole stone heavier. Love handles lick over the edge of my jean belt. My cheeks look like I have bits of cotton wool stored in them—just like with a hamster. I even walk a little funny as my thighs are starting to rub together and I now realise why fat people have adopted a certain wobble. Despite my fat status I did manage to get laid last night. I picked up a fat girl as I wanted to know how it felt fucking in between all those layers of fat. It wasn't too bad. Not as bad as I thought it would be. I was unfaithful to Luisa, but if she was watching she would laugh, for the girl I picked wasn't attractive. Not like Alison Moyet or Dawn French with their beautiful, round features. No, this woman was just fat. When you are fat and having sex, you sweat more, and as we were doing it our flesh squeaked as we slapped against each other. The girl was a bit out of breath, but I don't think that was down to my performance as my out-of-touch hips found it hard to wind and grind. Maybe I will have to fulfil my occasional need. God knows I hate wanking. I think it will be a nice way to die. Fat woman aren't that bad. I'm nearly a fat man. Give me another six months and I will be a plump, roly-poly pig.

My plans are going well. I am on full benefits and any job interviews don't end up with a job. They make you go on them as part of the getting-back-to-work scheme. It's easy, you just turn up in your scruffiest jeans, fart a lot, and complain of shortness of breath. I don't think you even need to do that. I've just got to be sure that I don't get the seven-to-seven job working in the condom factory, or the street cleaning job, or even the night watchman position. Fat people are discriminated against without having to put on the act. Fat people are seen as disease. I do think it is wrong; I really do, but I could lose weight if I want to. I just don't want to. Rachel's gloating face is staring back at me with every mouthful of food that I take. *Go for it, big boy. Go on, I dare you. I double dare you.* She laughs as my fat hands hold my dick and I can just about squeeze into the bathroom to take a piss. My arse broke the toilet seat the other week. I now have an inflatable cushion one. I'm starting to develop bedsores or what I imagine bedsores to be. Red, raised or spotty marks line the inside of my thighs and gnat bites that I got in the summer are still there. My body can't heal like it used to. I have to take the lift now even though I only live on the second floor. Just getting in and out of it leaves me out of breath. All my benefits go on my food bills. I would eat more if wasn't for the fact that my cousin has confiscated my last ten grand. He won't give it to me. He knows I would just spend the lot on cakes.

My next door neighbour, Pat, is a kind, fit, fifty-nine-year-old and she has the Internet. She doesn't have anyone, either. She always wears red slippers; red slippers and green tracksuits. They are made of that awful velour stuff. You know the stuff that grannies wear. She isn't a granny, but she wears the cheap velour stuff as she can't really afford anything else. She apparently got pregnant at seventeen and dedicated her life to bringing up her boy alone. She's not sure who the father was. Well, this kid gave her meaning, then one day he takes a short cut home across the railway tracks and ends up being decapitated after his foot gets stuck in the track. She hasn't been the same since and that was years ago. She's a nice lady and she lets me use the computer once a week to order my shopping. Now I don't even have to leave the house much.

"Eric, you should go and see the doctor, get him to wire your mouth shut. If you aren't careful, then a heart attack will get you soon." She means it, but her concern nearly makes me laugh,

"I bloody hope so—I really do," I whisper, but I have never been one to have such luck. Some people just aren't favoured, I guess.

Why Rachel Broke My Balls
March '98

The press chase us for half a mile. I just want it to be normal every once in a while. That's a lie, as I want to be normal most days. This fame thing was great for the first year when I was on TV and went to the Brit awards and fucked lots of beautiful woman. It was fun when I ordered my first Aston Martin, which I wrapped around a tree in less then a month of owning it. Jay, as in Jamiroquai, invited me over to race him on his homemade race track. That guy can drive. I wasn't so hot and then after skidding round a corner had a lucky escape when the thing crashed into a tree. All I could think about when his marshals pulled me out of there was about that poor Rebecca and how her parents felt. It was good that day until that point. Still, there are no worries as I just brought another one! I didn't race it again, though, as I kind of lost my bottle that day. Wimp—limp boy that I am.

It was great when I won a Grammy. James and the Orange Men sold like hotcakes over in the States. I got the Grammy for it and then all the stars in America wanted to invite me over for dinner. It was wonderful when I met Madonna for the first time and she asked me to work with her on her next album. It was hard work, but people still hailed it the best album of her career. I still get plenty of phone calls and job offers. I do some of them, of course, but now that I have Rachel, work comes second to her. We have brought our first place jointly. I don't want to say how much it's costing us!

Where we were living beforehand, in my old place, I couldn't even go onto the balcony. The press were that bad. I needed to get milk last week and there must have been someone camped outside our place in a car, as it was eight o'clock on a Sunday morning. We both felt like shit. We keep doing too much drugs, doing too much drink. Mixing and fixing and not getting enough sleep. I was tired, but we needed to eat. We were going to eat, have a shag, then sleep as Rachel was going off for a few days with work. That's why we moved, as I don't want to be snapped scratching my arse in the street with nothing more than sweats on. I only wanted milk. Why the hell should I do my hair to go and buy milk if I'm only going to go straight back to bed? Maybe I should have worn shades, for that is what Rachel said. She said my eyes wouldn't have looked so bad if I had done the shades thing, but it was pissing down with rain and I would have felt a bit of a tit parading about the street with "Police" sunglasses on in the rain.

Rachel loves it. Love that is counted as being so special. It's a bit superficial, but it is a good life. She has calmed me down a lot. She thinks that maybe I have calmed down too much. She hasn't seen me out with Eddy, then. Eddy always has to carry me home when we go out together. I don't want Rachel to see me like that. She may think it would be fun, but she would hate me for it. The papers would have a field day. She couldn't carry me home, for one thing. She has me where she wants me, though. Squeezed right between her thighs, unable to escape, just as she likes it.

The papers do seem to live like shadows around us. I wonder if she rings them in advance to say that we are on our way, as they always seem to know where to find us. Rachel, always holding my hand. That is very important, she tells me, that if they see us out and we aren't hold hands then they will think we have had a tiff. Occasionally, she tells me that.

"No matter how hard I feel like holding your hand today, Eric, we can't, we need the press."

"I hate all that shit, babe."

"Eric, trust me," she says. I always do. So when we get out of the car at the latest *Star Wars* premier and she has a sultry, moody look which says that it's just all getting too much for her, and I face the other way, well, I don't like doing this, but the next day we are on the cover of every gossip magazine. A few nights later we will normally go out to the Ivy or some other high profile place; this week it's the Ivy. We sit opposite each other in our spring bests and she tells me, "Eric, you're not to take your hands off me. We are going to be so all over each other in this restaurant that people will think we are deeply in love."

"But we are, aren't we?" I ask, scared by how easily this comes to her.

"Yes, but we have to work with it, Eric. Let them really know this."

"I don't need to pretend, Rachel."

"Then we will have no problem convincing them, then, will we?" she says, smiling, not picking up on my pain and I thought girls were supposed to be the sensitive ones.

I drop it, though, as she won't get it, or at least pretends not to and all that will happen is that an argument will burn in the pot.

Halfway through the meal she makes me follow her into the ladies. People's heads do turn and a clicker of low voices spit behind us. We don't do anything in there; I don't even get a shag out of it, but we make the papers all right. I force a redundant kiss out of her … it's as if she can't be bothered when no one is watching. She's a minx.

*

Today is a Monday morning and all I want to do is just go and get some furniture—a new bed and stuff. We aren't at a premier or anything else, so I can't see why we shouldn't get peace and quiet. But even this will make the papers, even if Rachel is also wearing sweats and her hair is nothing more than a ponytail and her perfect face merely dusted with a stroke of blusher. They don't care; they want her no matter how she looks. She is beautiful and tells me that, "it looks good, Eric, if a celebrity is occasionally pictured looking natural. It makes her seem more human to the ordinary people, more accessible."

"Why can't we just have one day alone?" I snap. "That wanker over there with the camera is really pissing me off."

"Don't be so rude to them, Eric. They already called you 'Arrogant Eric.'"

"Well, sweetheart, we only did a press conference the other day. Can't we shop in peace? They just wind me up so much these days."

"Posh and Becks can't, so I don't see why we should! It never used to bother you. Remember, they pay our meal tickets!"

"We are hardly Posh and Becks!" I say, turning to wipe a piece of fluff from her face. She smiles as I gently stroke her face. They will have photographed that.

"Not long, my dear, not long," she says, turning her chest toward the photographer.

"I don't know if I want that, Rachel." She ignores my comments and grins as a camera flash snaps.

"Get away," I tell the man, leading Rachel by the hand into Harrods. Good old Harrods, the security stop the press from following us. It's worth it to pay their prices just for that.

Rachel has the most expensive taste that I have ever known. The girl would spend all her money if it wasn't for me helping her out. I spoil her, I know, but she deserves it. The earrings I bought her last week look good. So do her freshly bleached teeth. I can see what she is saying; you really do need to have good teeth in this industry, but the gum shield she wears in bed makes her look like a boxer and it's a bit of a passion killer lately.

We have only been here half an hour and already, for the life of me, I don't know how, but we have already blown nearly a hundred grand on a bed! It's £86,999, to be precise. It's only for sleeping on. On a bed, for God sake! I didn't even like it. It's too fussy. It's what Eddy calls tacky-rich, what with its over-the-top, built-in satin headboard and its decadent swans carved into the legs and posts. There is even gold leaf on the decoration. Sweeping the cracks like gold bubble gum. The plain brown one in the corner for twenty grand is much nicer. Still bloody expensive, but far better then the crap we have just bought. The brown one is subtle, laid back and something that I can imagine myself in, Rachel wrapped up next to me.

"What about the brown one?" I ask, but Rachel turns up her nose.

"Too manly, Eric," she says, dragging the happy shop assistant over to the matching bedroom furniture.

"That's a shame," I say, but no one is really listening. The way Rachel sees it is that it isn't any good if it doesn't have a big price tag on it. She does the same with wine and everything else we buy.

"Thank you, Miss Garbo, Mr. Morrison." The store manager must have heard about the big sale and comes over to make sure that we are being looked after. "Please call me—here is my card, should you have any questions or problems."

"Why, thank you!" Rachel says, sounding and looking again a bit like Scarlet O'Hara.

I am fed up now; this place is doing my head in. She just won't stop shopping. How much of this stuff do you really need?

"Come on, sulky," she says, pulling me from the easy chair that I have been glued to since she disappeared off to bedding. "We are going."

"Oh, that's a shame!" I say, as she hands me a bill for four hundred grand!

"How much!" I say.

"Don't spoil it, Eric," she says, nipping my arm coldly, "we needed these things for our new place. If it's going to be joint venture, then I just want everything new."

"I give up," I say, as we smile for the photographs outside. Our new pad is in Knightsbridge, which I think is a bit pompous and old, but Rachel says that since she was a little kid she has wanted to live in Knightsbridge.

"Now that wasn't too bad, was it?" she asks me over a glass of champagne at the bar in Sugars, a trendy new restaurant. A place so trendy that it doesn't have tablecloths, its glasses are made out of ice and all the staff look like they have just walked out of a *Vogue* photo shot. Pretty people, so pretty that they give even the most attractive woman a run for her money. If you aren't rich, then you won't even be able to buy a glass of tap water in this place, not that anyone would ever be vulgar enough to drink tap water here. I just want a chicken sandwich, but that isn't going to happen here—it's far too posh to serve chicken. I have steak in the end and Rachel has lobster. She looks embarrassed when they bring it as she's not sure how she should be eating it. She turns her head. No one is watching her and she mutters, "I don't know what to do!"

"Just eat it. Use that thing there. Yes, there. It just breaks up the shell." She messes it up at first and tries not to laugh. I am only laughing as I know how important it is to her. I am being cruel. She starts laughing as well. I knew she couldn't keep it up for long.

"Damn this lobster!" she says, giving up and learning over to take a bite out of my steak.

"Rachel, do you even like it?"

"I don't know. I'm getting nothing but mouthfuls of shell," she says, flicking her black hair from her face with nails of red.

"You are a funny bird."

"I'm having dessert then. I'm starving."

"Can I at least finish my sandwich and wine before you start to eye up the desserts menu?"

"Sure, don't worry, it takes me ages to decide." Someone comes to fill our glasses. The champagne is going down too easily.

"Another bottle, sir?" the Brad Pitt lookalike waiter asks.

"Yes," Rachel butts in. "Can we have some French fries as well?"

He totters off and I see Rachel watching his backside! I thought woman weren't supposed to be interested in stuff like this. He *has* got a better backside than me, but still, the girl is so obvious. If I did that she would give me a slap straight around the face!

"So when's all our stuff arriving?" I ask, feeling the heat from my credit card burning though my wallet and into my leg. It is scarring my flesh and my bank manager is bouncing up and down on his leather chair. He is going to wack up the bank charges on my account.

"It will be there tomorrow. So I guess we will just have to slob it for one more night at your place."

"Sod it! My flats great."

"If you say so, Eric." She laughs. "Now, when he comes back, get him to get me some chocolate torte with ice cream." She winks, running off to take a crap. I know she is, as she won't go around me. The way she sees it, if she uses a public toilet in a posh place like this no one will notice. Funny girl.

Why am I with her? She is sticking to my every action. Her pale, porcelain skin and those fiery green eyes—I have to admit that she's the only girl who I haven't got sick of doing it with. I could ride her for eternity. Even when she grows past it I reckon she will be a good lay. She's honest, also. She doesn't pretend that she doesn't want to make it. She shows she cares about stuff like that and I suppose it is better than faking it. She does have some depth; you just have to get to know her to discover so.

"Rachel, lets go home and fuck," I say as she finishes her dessert. I like to be crude with her.

"But I want a coffee."

"I've got a five hundred pound coffee machine indoors—we can have it at home."

"OK, it has been a long day—but can we get a take in for dinner, then?"

"Yes, babe." I laugh—Rachel always lives in the future, she has no past, and only skips in and out of the present. The future is the only way she is prepared to live. Not a very healthy way to live, but she has dynamite sticks under her feet and they don't seem to bore of exploding.

She is wearing Victoria's Secret, an American underwear range that is guaranteed to turn men to putty. Oh, and I am her putty tonight. She can mould me into whatever she wants to. Her white skin isn't sickly pale like some girls, but rather a pretty pale like Marilyn and that bird from No Doubt. Scarlet knickers frame her hips and match the ruby in her stomach. With her black hair she is my Scarlet O'Hara, my temptress. I don't think I love her. For I could not have the thoughts I am having right now if I was in love with her. I can't help it, I'm imagining a million different ways to fuck her. I feel greedy, like I want to do them all, but I am getting so excited that there is no way I'll get past just one of the positions. I have to calm down. Think of women in tabards, grannies in the bath. Fat birds in the rain. Anything to stop it happening too soon! The grannies won't stay in my head, and I see Rachel in a nun's dress. It's shorter then the real ones, but she has a habit on. She holds her scarlet finger up to her scarlet mouth and tells me to be quiet, to trust her to follow what she is doing. It nearly happens again. OK, the Granny in the bath thing, then, but I can't imagine anything but beauty at the moment. Come on, Eric, you used to eat woman like this up for snacks! Think of all the nice girls you have had over this bed! You chewed woman for fun until she came along! After we had finished I would ask them to go. I don't need Rachel, I don't, but, well, oh my God, I want her more than anything.

"Are you OK, Eric?" she asks me, taking my hands to her breasts. I undo the strap at the back and they rest into my grip. I am sad. She's under my skin and I don't think I will ever be able to dig her out. She knows I won't last long and she takes her pants off and we are off.

I last longer than I expected to. Longer than the first time I saw her in the flesh.

"We are good together, we are so good together," she tells me as we hug each other on my bed.

"Rachel you are so …"

"What," she says, as I move her hair from her face and kiss her.

"You are just great."

"You, too, Eric. You are the first guy I have trusted, the first guy to live up to what he has promised me. I need you, Eric, I need you so much."

She kisses my chest and disappears off into the bathroom, her black hair waving down her back, her round arse bouncing gently like bra-ed bosoms.

After that moment I was gone, one hundred percent wearing my blind mother fucker glasses. I had thought I was happy—that Rachel could reach me on another level that other women had failed. The only thing that had failed was my ability to see when I was being used. Even the sex was an act with Rachel—she just homed in on what I like, what made me tick. She used me, then kicked me into the bottom of the deepest trench she could find.

Feeble Fat Maker

Fuck, you have become a fatty! Your skin would clearly gain you employment at some fast food chain! I tell myself as I pull a stray hair from my nose. *You are now one of the ugly ones. You are so fat now that you can't even pull fat birds, you can't even pull the dogs!* My feet are no longer visible if I look down at them whilst using the clip-on shower head. I have to use twice as much shower gel these days as, despite the foam, my sweat seems to stick to me like honey to bread. Even my underpants are like tents. I buy black ones, as white ones stain too easily. Just getting in and out of the bath is an effort, that's why I stand and shower. It takes me an hour to wash and dress. That's fine, as I don't really have much else to do with my time.

Today I am going to take some flowers to Luisa's grave. We buried her in England, as I didn't know what else to do and she always did like that big graveyard at Stoke Newington. Maybe I should have sent her back to Spain, but no one asked me to. Her mother came over here for the service and she didn't speak a word of English. Well, the only thing she did say was that I was a good boy. I'm glad I'm not famous in her country. I'm pleased that she just thought I was a nobody. It kind of fits.

The woman from upstairs asked me to turn my TV down the other night. I felt really bad. She works as a nurse and I had fallen asleep with it full-pelt. She told me that she nearly gave someone the wrong medication due to being so tired! I feel bad—I don't want to be seen as a killer! I could make it a hat trick, then, and go down in history as "The Man Who Didn't Mean To."

I will get some headphones on my way back today so that if I want to watch it late at night I won't disturb the nurse. Imagine that, imagine all the training she has gone through, the shiny degree she got, and to end up in a shit hole with the likes of me just because the government won't pay her enough to even be able to get onto the property market! That sucks! She was so nice when I explained that I had fallen asleep. She didn't even mention my size. Most people mention my size. She didn't.

I make an effort and buy a Christmas bouquet from Sainsbury's. There is holly, mistletoe and lots of green and white flowers. I take a taxi to the graveyard. I have enough money put by to do so. The taxi driver doesn't talk to me and I don't talk to him. There isn't much traffic out today. But some stupid motorcyclist nearly gets himself killed. Those couriers, it has been rumoured, only do about seven runs before they are killed. I'm sure that isn't true, but it could be since this guy in front nearly got hit by us.

"Can I let you out here, mate?" the taxi driver asks. "It's just there are road works down the road and if I get stuck in them and I'm late to take my daughter to the airport, then my wife will kill me. She's flying off to India today and I would like to say goodbye."

"Sure," I say, amazed that this man has told me his whole life story. A simple, "Can I let out here?" would have done. It's because I am fat. I just know it is. He thinks I have no friends, wouldn't mind a spot of light conversation. He's right, of course.

My arse wobbles as I walk now. Wobble, shake, wobble … everyone knows when I am coming down the street. Sweat crowns my head through the cold. This is the most walking I have done all year. The graveyard is endless; well, in the snow it appears that way. I remember the way, though, for how could I forget that cold, wet day? It always rains at funerals on the television and the same could be said on that day.

Fresh snow covers her grave. I like the snow. Its pureness is enough to bring a tear to my eye. It's come early as Christmas is still two weeks away. Oh, Christmas ... this isn't going to happen for me this year, now is it. It's a stupid holiday if you ask me. Still ... still, I will be there all alone with my three Marks and Spencer dinners, a chocolate log, mince pies, and I'll spend my time watching TV re-runs and gulping my twelve-pack of lager. I have already selected the three cans of sweets I am going to have. I have even bought myself a present. It might sound stupid, but I sent an e-mail to Amazon asking them to make me a selection for £50.00. A surprise going on the past things I have bought. I thought they might laugh at me—that some stupid employee would email me back telling me that there was no way that this could happen, but they didn't. Well, they did email me, but only to tell me that they would send it gift-wrapped free of charge, as I have given them a wonderful idea for anyone who doesn't have anyone! That's me all right ... Billy No Mates. Glad I could bring a smile to the other friendless, childless, family-less people of this world.

I have it already sitting underneath my cactus. I have even hooked a bit of tinsel onto the cactus. It reminds me of Luisa. I know she isn't Mexican, but they all speak Spanish there and apart from orange trees (which I know they have in Spain), I'm not sure what plants they have out there since I haven't been to Spain before.

"No wonder you want to move to Spain," Her mother said in Spanish as her brown skin shivered in the wind as we waited to give Luisa to the ground.

"No wonder, indeed, and now I am stuck here in a cold, wet, living nightmare."

"What?" she asked, but I smiled and led her to her taxi.

The grave has no flowers. This is sad for someone so freshly laid to its grounds. My blood-red roses, mixed into my Christmas bouquet, look surreal against the grey and white ground. I try not to stand on the mound. I like the way the snow is blanketing her grave, protecting her like a big quilt. She would be ashamed if she could see me. I hope she can't. I want her to be happy. Maybe there is a nice

Spanish boy for her to meet in heaven. Maybe she has long forgotten me. How I want to join her. I hope really that there isn't a nice Spanish boy, but maybe a nice friend or grandmother to look after her would be good. It's in my nature to be selfish ... I always have been.

Now I have come all the way over here, I don't feel like staying for long. It's cold, being here has done little more than make me feel upset. I really miss her, you know—more than anything. I cry a little. It doesn't matter, no one is around. The snow is coming down heavy and it's difficult to see where I am. The gate is in the distance, but snow flakes are attacking my face. Each one of them is Luisa, duplicated into an infinite number. A frowning Luisa, a disappointed Luisa, a let-down Luisa, a happy Luisa, a sad Luisa, an I'm-not-sure Luisa, etc. I think she wants to drown me deep beneath the snow. My body disgusts her. My body repulses her.

"Eric, you have let me down," she says. I run so hard I don't realise I have reached the main road. I run into a stationary car. I am unlucky, as I am not killed because the traffic lights are red.

"Watch it, you fat bastard!"

"Sorry," I say as the little man with jam jar glasses waves his puny fist at me.

"Fuck off," I say in the end; contemplating whether or not to sit on his car, even to sit on him until he is as flat as freshly rolled pastry. I don't do this, of course; I want to, but I don't. I want to ring his neck, but I don't. I am lucky today as a taxi is coming my way.

"I'm only going south, mate!" he yells at me through the window as if being fat will suddenly make me hard of hearing.

"Well, it's your lucky day," I say, "because so am I."

The bastard journey takes forever and for the first time in ages I have actual hunger pains. Feed me, fat bastard, feed me. My stomach tells me again and again. Now, now. I want to be fed. I should have bought headphones, but I'm out of the shopping mood. I'll just turn the sound right down on the TV and get them tomorrow.

I get in and I want cakes, and fatty chicken, all coated in batter. I want Indian takeaway or even Chinese. The excitement of which menu to pick has to be delayed as I take a pee. My hands are so cold that I'm sure my piss is going to turn into one great long icicle. I could save it and enter it as art into that Turner prize.

The mirror eggs me to take a look. I am Eric Morrison and I am a loser. A bit of me is still here, but I'm in someone's body. No one knows who I am. I'm Eric Morrison, once the greatest record producer and now nothing more than a food junkie. I don't contribute anything to society. I don't contribute anything to my own life. I don't have a point.

I go for the Chinese set menu for two with extra prawn crackers. The food doesn't touch the sides. I eat every last grain of rice, every last crumb and sauce splash. My plate is clean. I want to order another one and would if it wasn't for the fact that I have no cash on me.

Time for a sleep. A big, long, deep sleep. … I'm too fat to get into bed; once I have eaten there is no moving me. So as the juices stew in my stomach, I stew on the sofa. I poach away like a chubby piece of pork, bubbling in a pot, cooking away into nothing more than decay.

Awakenings

The next morning I hear bells. I'm on some beach somewhere when someone comes up to my ear and starts to ring in it. Like those handheld bells you sometimes see.

"What!" I say when I realise it's the postman. Fred's a stubborn git. Most postmen ring the bell once and then leg it before you even get a chance to get there. Not Fred, he will ring and ring until you have no choice than to go and answer it.

"All right, all right!" I shout, struggling to the door.

"Got a parcel for you today!" he says, sparkly, despite it being seven in the morning. "Looks like something exciting," he adds, his yellow beard is the only thing that separates him as something different from the old *Jim Will Fix It* presenter, that and his postman's uniform.

"Thanks," I say, slamming the door by accident. The parcel isn't something I have ordered. I have stopped the mail order stuff, as it's getting expensive. The parcel smells like lemons. Maybe they have started doing scented paper. More than likely the idea came over from the States. The parcel, however, is Spanish. I can tell by the postal stamp. Luisa and her mother used to write to each other. The parcel looks like it's from her mother, as the writing is the same. It's been wrapped with care and I need the scissors to open it. Lemons tumble everywhere! Fat, juicy, oversized lemons, unwaxed and with wisps of greenery still attached to their cores. Dancing and tumbling onto my floor, I try my best to catch them.

There is also a letter and a bottle of deep Spanish wine packed into so much bubble wrap that it would be impossible to break. ... The letter is sitting on a box of biscuits. I have that box as my pre-breakfast snack. They taste homemade and are also flavoured with bits of lemon in them. The letter is in Spanish, but I can read it. It's from Luisa's mother.

> *Dear Eric*
>
> *I hope you are doing OK without Luisa. I know she is buried in London, but I have a feeling that she is really here with me in Spain. I miss her, Eric, and I miss getting to know you like I should have. I need your help, Eric, for I have become very old. I am not dying or anything as bad as that, but I am not going to be around forever. Luisa told me how well you run the restaurant in the UK and that's what I need to talk to you about.*
>
> *I can't afford to live here any longer without opening it up. My son doesn't want to do it and my other daughter has a family and can only work part-time. I love this house, the lemon groves, and the people. I have lived here for forty years now and I just can't bear to leave it. Eric, would you consider coming over here and being my manager? I know you have picked up Spanish quite well from the conversation I had with you when I came to visit and also from what Luisa used to say. I need someone I can trust, you see.*
>
> *You are young, fit and I guess finding it hard to find a purpose.*
>
> *Let me know.*
>
> *Maria*
>
> *X*

I don't know what to say. She is asking a lot. I'm fat now. I bet she wouldn't have written me if she knew how fat I was. I will not be able to do anything. I can't even walk down the road without getting out of breath. The woman in the cake shop gives me free cakes if I decide to go out. I used to give her so much business. I was once the greatest record producer the world has ever known. Now I'm frightened of a future. Why did Maria have to go and write to me? I had it all mapped out … the middle right through to the dramatic end. I can't change things now. The lemons, their smell; they smell like summer.

To take my mind off any big decisions, I cook myself a big fry up of sausages, streaky bacon, three fried eggs and a pot of beans. I have nearly half a loaf buttered to mop and slop the juices. I never waste food. Never.

Bewitched is starting on channel four. I always watch *Bewitched* with breakfast nowadays. My food looks great, but after the first mouthful I feel sick. I stagger to the bathroom and I'm sick. Last night's curry stares back up at me from the bottom of the pan. I don't think I can do this anymore. I stink. I stink so bad that it doesn't matter how many times I wash myself, I still stink.

I had a plan and now I am confused. That woman doesn't even know me and to expect me to drop everything just because she might lose her home. I've lost a lot more. A lot more than she has!

Bewitched finishes. This is the time when I am most lost in the day. There isn't anything on until *This Morning* starts. I flick with hope and do find a holiday program with warm, beating sun to warm up my eyes. It is a dark Irish guy presenting it and he's in Seville. It looks beautiful and all the women look like my Luisa. I miss her. The sun is just like a juicy orange, just like Luisa had said it was. Their world looks so different to mine. So beautiful and full of warmth. I look around my dismal room. The whole place is dismal—London can be dismal unless you have lots of cash. It's like a good lover with a bad personality, you know it's not right for you, but it is very hard to give up. Now, however, I am ready to give her up since her deterioration—I can't do this anymore. I have been kidding myself to pretend that I can. I hate this shit. I have wasted the last year or so of my life getting fat. I thought it would be the right thing and then this happened and now I know I have been acting the fool. I am rarely this impulsive. I have made my mind up and I can't be fat anymore. This has only happened to me a couple times in my life—the first time was the day I got my first break in the music business. I just had a feeling all night as I d.j.'d the gig of my life. I just knew I had been spotted. My mate Tiger said I was imagining it, but I wasn't—my sound system was plugged into the universe and a favour was heading right my way. The same thing happened when Luisa and I decided to move to Spain—I knew it was the right thing—it would have been. How was I to also know that the devil also had plans for us? He won this time, this battle, but I won't give him the war.

* * * * *

Six months later I arrive in Seville. I have lost a stone, but still have a long way to go. I've left most of my stuff behind. It is my past now and unless I can detach myself from it I will never make it into the future. I'm not sure that I have to forget it, though, for it has made me who I am. A fat bastard, yes—but one who now has a tiny inch of hope.

My cousin weakened—he gave me the last of my money. After all, I could be dead next week or I might even live for another fifty years. Life is like that, cruel and kind at the same time.

They welcome me like a son. They don't blame me for Luisa. I would blame me.

"Come sit, Eric," they say as I am given a wonderful dinner with Luisa's mother and the rest of the family in their lemon-scented garden. The fat orange sun is calming as we sip *Rioja* and gently bake in its evening rays. Her mother speaks little English, but she has invited her ten-year-old nephew to translate. There is no need as I can get by in Spanish.

This is how it would be if Luisa and I had had our dream. She always said to me that her mother's homemade desserts were good enough to wake the dead, but Luisa isn't here, for she is at rest now, being re-born into some wonderful kingdom.

Maria and I go over the plans for opening up the restaurant/music venue. She tells me that, "Eric, I am far too old—but my niece can help you. I will teach her to cook and you can do the rest."

Luisa's little nephew interprets badly and I wink and slip him a coin. I love him and everyone already. People like this give me hope. They are like Luisa and take me as I come. They don't judge or bitch, but are kind, caring, and I really do believe these people have the purist souls I have ever met.

It does work out in the end. I'm not saying that I have sailed into a happy ending, for I haven't. Despite the friendship and the way I am treated as one of their family, I don't feel fully complete. It's after the restaurant closes and in that time between morning and dawn I am at my most lonely and often feel as if I could have made a big mistake. But business is good, I have friends, and I'm aiming to one day be able to sleep all night without taking a pill. I think I will stick here for a while and give it a go. Put it this way, it's a damn sight better than living where I used to.

So, now that you have heard my tale, does your group still empathise with it? Do you get my point? Do you understand the problem I used to have? I know I'm not totally cured, but I think it's starting to go away. I have made a life now, the only regret is that I didn't take a chance earlier and leave when Luisa was still around. Pride is a funny thing.

Anyway, I'm sure you all have homes to get back to, so I won't keep you … but just remember this, addiction is a nasty disease, but it can be treated. I have been lucky, I am not going to deny that. Yes, despite my tragedy, I could have sank right to the bottom of despair, but since I have been given a second chance I've made damn sure that this time I haven't ignored it, that I didn't let it slip away.

I hope you have learnt something today and that you can go away from this help group with a positive attitude about your future.

I have to go now. Have a great day.

Printed in the United Kingdom
by Lightning Source UK Ltd.
103745UKS00001B/47

9 781413 763546